The Dark Descent Copyright © 2018 by Jerry Knaak

Trifecta Publishing House

All rights reserved. Except as permitted under the U.S. Copyright Act of 1976, no part of this publication may be reproduced, distributed, or transmitted in any form or by any means now known or hereafter invented, or stored in a database or retrieval system, without the prior written permission of the publisher, Trifecta Publishing House.

This book is a work of fiction Names, characters, places, and incidents are the product of the author's imagination or are used fictitiously. Any resemblance to actual persons, living or dead, business establishments, events, or locales is coincidental.

Published in the United States of America First Printing: 2018

Print

ISBN -13: 978-1-943407-45-3

E-Book

ISBN -13: 978-1-943407-46-0

Trifecta Publishing House

1120 East 6th Street

Port Angeles, Washington

98362

TRIFECTA PUBLISHING HOUSE

Contact Information: Info@TrifectaPublishingHouse.com

Editor: Elizabeth Jewell

Cover Art by Rae Monet

Formatted by Monica Corwin

THE DARK DESCENT

Book Two - The Dark Passage Series

JERRY KNAAK

For William

CHAPTER I

When you're trapped in an abandoned coal mine at Land's End, you'd think you would have plenty of time for reflection, contemplation, introspection, and self-evaluation. Even after your eyes have adjusted and the initial rage that gives way to eventual acceptance has subsided, you'd think you'd be able to center yourself and try to understand your existence.

Most people would try to find water and sustenance. Most people would worry about running out of air. Most people would be frantically clawing and digging at the rock and dirt that entrapped them. Most people would fear death, resign themselves to it, or even welcome it.

I am not most people.

After my last hissy fit and my most recent tantrum directed at the large boulder that blocked the entrance to—my exit from—the long-forgotten coal mine under Deadman's Point—more irony—I was overcome by a calm I had not known in life. I leaned against the rock standing between me and freedom and thought long and hard about the past few months. My last evening in the fresh sea air was of particular interest to me.

The San Francisco Police Department's Detective Sergeant Jonas Dietrich was probably being grilled by his superiors. What did he know, and how long had he known it? Why was he with me on the beach at the Sutro Baths when the SWAT team directed by his colleague came storming down the hillside, guns blazing? I wondered if he still had his position with the San Francisco Police Department at all.

I had looped a heavy chain around Andrei's neck and dumped his pompous ass into an adjacent lagoon. Was the pretentious prick still alive, or had I finished my maker, once and for all? The realization that he had tormented me since I was twelve was a splinter in my brain. It was an itch I couldn't scratch. I had finally confronted this … this thing. And I had won. Nobody had believed me when I had talked about the face in the window … the figure in my bedroom … but I hadn't been hallucinating. I hadn't been imagining things. I'd been fucking right, goddammit. Fat lot of good that was doing me now.

The connection between Andrei and Dietrich was mind-blowing. What were the odds? Did Andrei really kill Dietrich's grandfather? Did the same fate await Jonas? Impossible; Andrei was gone. I'd made sure of that. "Did I? Did I really? I don't know, dammit, I just don't know." My words echoed as I ran my fingers through what was left of my hair and pulled hard on the ends.

What I *did* know was that my best friend was dead. Julie Engstrom wasn't coming back. Andrei had made sure of that. That scene on the beach was seared into my retinas. Julie naked, crucified, and bled out, sputtering her last words as she passed. Her death was so unnecessary; pointless. Andrei had killed her out of spite. This whole sordid episode had started with her invitation to go to the club. If I had stuck to my proclivities and gone home that night, none of this would have happened. I would have gotten lost in a good book and a bottle of merlot, or maybe even a game of kick the cat, and I would have been Public Relations Professional of the Year by now.

Oh, who the hell was I kidding? Those were delusional thoughts. Andrei had "marked" me, chosen me, targeted me since I was an adolescent—sick fuck—and there's no way he would have given me up. Yeah, there'd been a gap of more than twenty years in his stalking, but he had found me again. What had happened that night at The Dark Truth was inevitable.

But then again, I wasn't exactly special, was I? I just fit a profile, a type. I was of a certain ethnicity with a hair color and a figure he liked. It was even more disgusting to know that he started these markings with young girls. Or was I different?

I was his "accident," for crying out loud. What did he

expect was going to happen? What did he think I was going to do? Did he really think in his black, decayed heart of hearts that I would just screw off into the night and not hunt him down?

I didn't give a flying fuck that I had brought the police down on his head. Why should I? He'd made me. He'd done this to me. He was responsible. He needed to pay and pay dearly. As much as it would have amused me to watch him suffer in a jail cell as he tried to reconcile his existence with incarceration, he'd gotten what he deserved: a miserable death by my hand.

Trying to find someone to blame was a pointless exercise. Andrei was responsible. Nobody else. And I had taken care of him. After Julie put me through that rotted sheetrock at the abandoned house at Moss Beach, I'd been surprised I had the wherewithal and the prowess to defeat Andrei in hand-to-hand combat. Perhaps it was pure luck or serendipity, but the heavy, rusty chain lying in the sand could not have been more convenient. I sincerely hoped my aversion to water was an accurate instinct and that the lagoon would serve as a watery grave for my maker.

CHAPTER II

When I wasn't turning over the events of the past few months in the saltwater taffy puller of my clouded and confused mind, I explored my rock and brick prison. The raccoons were lousy company, although I was a bit relieved to know I was sharing the mine with something other than rats and this maddening thirst. The furry, masked bandits spent almost as much time as I did trying to find a way out of this hell. I wondered if they would turn to cannibalism when the supply of rats was exhausted or if they'd eventually turn on me. *"Bring it, you little bastards."*

My ability to see in relative darkness had proven to be invaluable, especially since I had decided to hide in this sorry excuse for a Scholomance. A school of black magic this was not. The random things I remembered from medieval folklore classes boggled my mind. I certainly wasn't gaining any knowledge of my condition trapped here in this network of caves and tunnels.

Since I'd proclaimed myself the Queen of Random Thoughts, an incredible array of memories, songs, and pop culture crackled across my synapses. As I explored one particularly large tunnel, I broke into a song and dance from *The Rocky Horror Picture Show*.

I channeled my inner Little Nell and recreated her tap dance from the *Time Warp* scene the best I could. As she did in the film, I tripped and fell. A couple of times.

The thirst was unlike anything I had ever experienced in life. Sure, I had gotten parched, dehydrated even, but this was different. This was a gnawing deep within my core. I'd had serious issues when I'd missed one night of feeding. Those folks at that boutique in Livermore had found out the hard way. After just one night, it became a hunger. And now? I felt like a drug addict jonesing for a fix. The shakes couldn't be far behind. I had no idea how long I had been in the mine.

As I rounded a corner into a narrower passage, I was dumbfounded by what I saw. Three raccoons were menacing an animal they had cornered against a rock wall. As I drew nearer, I could make out the shape of the intended victim. Pointy ears, s-curved spine, long tail ... it was a cat. A fucking cat. *My cat.*

Blackfoot was at the mercy of three masked hooligans.

Her back was up, fur standing straight up, and her tail was poofed out five times bigger than normal. She was hissing and growling like I'd never heard. That damn cat was making sounds that I didn't know any creature in the animal kingdom was capable of uttering. I had thought the raccoons were howling and shrieking, but no, it was Blackfoot.

At first, I didn't know what to do. It took several seconds for the scene in front of me to register. The raccoon closest to my no-account cat leapt at her. I caught the attacker in midair and swung it. I slammed it into the rock as hard as I could, and it practically exploded on impact. Fur and bone smashed, and blood splattered as I made a cave painting out of the thing. I positioned myself between Blackfoot and the two hissing, fuzzy desperados that remained. They hunched down and paced back and forth as they sized me up. The one to my immediate right jumped high while its partner dove at my ankles.

My left leg shot out instinctively; my foot caught the critter square in its midsection and launched it across the tunnel. It uttered a pained squeal as it struck the rock with a sickening crunch. Blackfoot sprang and tackled the high flyer before it could hit me. The feline and the raccoon hit the ground and rolled in a life-or-death tussle. I waited until I had a window, then reached out and grabbed the would-be cat killer by the tail. I swung it over my head like a lariat before I finally slammed it repeatedly into the dirt floor of the passage. I probably took a few more swings than I needed to, but I was working some stuff out. And fuck, was I thirsty.

I tossed the carcass aside and scooped Blackfoot into my arms. A quick examination confirmed that she was just fine; nary a scratch. She was missing a little fur here and there, but no blood had been drawn. It didn't take her long to start purring like a sports car and nuzzling me.

Blackfoot curled up in my lap as I slid to the ground and rested against the rock wall. I gently scratched her between the ears and rubbed under her chin, much to her delight. I had grown accustomed to this vagabond showing up in the strangest places since the … turning. Then, it hit me.

"What the fuck are you doing here, cat? How the hell did you find me? Never mind that; how in holy hell did you get in here?" I half expected an answer. A gentle mew was the only reply.

She didn't get in by way of the beach entrance. That was blocked up. Was there a vein or a tunnel I hadn't found? Well, she wasn't Lassie, so I didn't exactly expect her to lead me out of the mine. But she'd gotten in here somehow. Never mind the weird psychic connection she had to me now. This damn cat couldn't be bothered with me before the … turning, and now, well, now, she wouldn't leave me the fuck alone. I was thankful, though. I had a spark of hope I didn't have before wrecking the raccoons.

After a long pause with my feline spelunker, I set her down and stood up. I thought I had explored every inch of this place. Every nook, every cranny, every craggy vein, artery, and passage; every shaft, every chimney—all for naught.

Blackfoot followed me as I explored. Twisting and turning, up a grade, down a slope, until I heard it.

CHAPTER III

"Helloooooooo! Anyone down therrrrrrrrre?"

It was a male voice. A familiar voice. It echoed off the walls of the mine, and I couldn't quite tell which direction it came from. I thought it sounded like Dietrich, but it couldn't be, could it?

"Hey! Help! Who's there?"

My voice disappeared down a tunnel that forked to the left, and I followed, with Blackfoot trailing behind me. I could hear the male voice getting louder and clearer as it continued to call out.

"Help! Help me!"

I could see light up ahead. It was dim, but it was brighter than any ambient light in the mine. My pace quickened as I moved toward the source of the illumination. I was pretty sure it wasn't a train.

"Elizabeth!"

It had to be Dietrich. Who else could it be? Nobody knew I was down here. Andrei was at the bottom of a lagoon, Julie was probably in the morgue, and it had been days since the SWAT team had chased me in here. My hope was that the cave-in had made them give up the search and leave me for dead. *More irony.*

This tributary was interminably long, but I was rewarded when I reached the end of it to find San Francisco Police Department Detective Sergeant Jonas Dietrich moving large rocks away as he tried to widen the hole where he'd entered. Blackfoot scooted past us and clambered out of the mine, her job done.

"Are you ever a sight for sore eyes, Jonas! How the hell …?"

"Not now. I'll explain everything later. Let's get you out of here."

Dietrich took my hand. I was struck by how cold his skin felt. What was that quote? *"The coldest winter I ever spent was a summer in San Francisco."* Now wasn't the time to worry about heat escaping from the detective's extremities. We climbed up and scrambled over rocks, large and small, until we emerged from the coal mine hell mouth and felt the cool summer night air hit our skin.

We stood above the mine and the ocean. It could have been a scene out of a Hollywood romantic comedy, only there was nothing romantic or funny about this nightmare.

"How?" I asked.

"Not now. C'mon, let's get out of here. My car's not far."

I was vaguely aware that he still held my hand and was now practically dragging me down a hill. I was weak with the thirst, my legs were rubber, and my mouth was desert dry.

"C'mon, not far."

"You said that already. Seriously, Jonas, what are we doing?"

"I know a place we can go and talk."

"I need to fee … " I stopped short. I knew he knew what I was. I knew he believed. He was there. He'd fought Andrei with me. He knew. But there was something off. There was something different about him. Something familiar.

"I know what you need."

Dietrich's standard issue midnight blue Crown Victoria sat idle in the USS San Francisco Memorial parking lot at the top of El Camino Del Mar. I tried the passenger side door only to find it locked. Dietrich opened the driver's side door and slid into the seat. He flicked a switch in the door handle and disengaged the lock for my door. In contrast, I clumsily fought the door and plopped into the passenger seat. I felt disoriented. The thirst had me. My eyes were about to roll back into my head. I felt like I could pass out.

"Here."

Dietrich casually tossed me a blood bag. I looked at it for a moment as if I didn't know what it was, like it didn't register. Then I tore into it like it was the flesh of a beast. I no sooner finished it before Dietrich tossed me another. Halfway through the second, I paused.

"It's cold. How did you … ?"

"Never you mind how."

As I savored the last half of the second bag of O positive, Dietrich inserted the key in the ignition and turned it over. The Crown Vic roared to life. We didn't say anything as I stared absentmindedly out the grimy, slimy windshield. Worn windshield wipers in dire need of replacement had smeared the only cleanish spots. The air inside the vehicle was heavy and thick with … something familiar, but I couldn't quite place it.

Dietrich put the car in gear and guided it out of the parking lot onto the road. Before long, we were headed south on 48th Avenue. He turned left on Balboa. Six and a half blocks later, we were parked again, this time behind an Egyptian restaurant that was closed for the night.

"Jonas, what are we doing?"

"Trust me."

I don't know why, but I kinda did. We closed the car doors simultaneously as we exited the vehicle. Dietrich quietly opened a service entrance in the back wall of the building, and we slipped inside. The proprietor greeted us in the kitchen.

"Good evening, Detective."

"Hello, Madu. How are you tonight?"

"I am well, my friend. Are you not going to introduce … ?"

"Oh, sorry. Madu, Elizabeth. Elizabeth, Madu."

"How do you do?"

"Very well, thank you."

"You'll find everything in the back-corner booth, Detective. And Jonas?"

"Yes, sir?"

"Lock up when you leave."

Dumbfounded, I followed Dietrich through the swinging double doors into the dining room. We took seats opposite each other. A pot of hot apple tea and a cup sat between stacks of Dietrich's case files. Some newer than others; some old, musty, and dusty. One item was achingly familiar. *My sketchbook.*

"How long was I in that mine?"

"Three days."

"It seemed like a lot longer than that."

"Well, not being able to sense the sunrise and sunset, one tends to lose track of time, especially folks like … "

He cut himself off before completing the sentence. Dietrich shuffled his files and papers and avoided eye contact. He once again slid my sketchbook between some dusty folders, not wanting to acknowledge his possession of it.

"So, how is it a San Francisco police detective comes to have after-hours access to an Egyptian eatery in Pacifica?"

"I helped Madu's son out of a beef once. Kid got jammed up. I got him out of it."

Dietrich sipped his apple tea as he finished the sentence.

"Must've been a pretty bad beef if he lets you in at all hours of the night."

"Yeah, well, I'm sure you've figured out that I don't keep what you would call normal hours."

"What happened after I went underground?"

Dietrich recounted the events of that night and told me about watching the SWAT team chase me toward the beach below Deadman's Point. An ambulance arrived shortly thereafter, and Julie was cut down from the makeshift crucifix at the Sutro Baths.

"Did she ... ?"

The detective stared at the table and shook his head before resuming his story. He told me that the SWAT team came back to the ruins fatigued and frustrated. They didn't stay long after the ambulance and CSI showed up.

"What did they say?"

"Not much. They said their search was fruitless and that shortly after they exited the mine, there was a cave-in."

I didn't want to ask my next question. I was deathly afraid of the answer.

"Andrei ... ?"

"No sign of him."

I slammed both fists down on the table, cracking the wood and upsetting the tea service.

"FUCK!"

I retreated into the corner of the booth like a scolded child when I saw the look on Dietrich's face. The disapproving scowl was enough to make me sheepish even though he was eighteen years my junior.

"What do you mean, *no sign?*" I whispered.

"I stayed as long as I could. I told everyone who would listen that there was a body at the bottom of that lagoon. They looked. I looked. A team of frogmen looked the next day. Nothing."

"You have got to be kidding me."

"I wish I were."

We talked some more. I told him about the mine system and what it was like to be trapped in there. He was surprised that I hadn't resigned myself and given up. I was more worried about madness than my expiration. What I couldn't quite figure was why I hadn't set upon him when he freed me. I'd had no desire to feed on Dietrich, as ravenous as I was at the time. Feeding was creeping into my mind again. The cold blood wasn't enough. And cold blood from a bag wasn't what I really needed. As I had experienced with the rats, only living human blood could really satisfy this ungodly thirst.

"Thank you, Jonas."

"Don't mention it. C'mon, it's going to be sunup soon, and we need to get you somewhere safe. And I just happen to know the spot."

Again, I didn't know why I trusted him. I just did. He packed up his materials, including my sketchbook, and locked the door as we left.

We drove deep into the heart of Pacifica until we

reached an abandoned chapel on the back side of the Sunset Reservoir. It was dark and decrepit. The outer walls were tagged by local graffiti artists; some skilled, some not so much.

Dietrich took me by the hand again and led me into the structure. He deftly navigated our way to a heavy oak door adjacent to the pulpit. A set of creaky wooden stairs led down. Dietrich took out a Zippo lighter and sparked sconces and candelabras mounted to the stone wall on the way to an underground crypt.

As we made our way through the pews and moved toward the side door, my eyes scanned the cathedral. It was devoid of almost all religious iconography. The crucifix was gone, the stained-glass windows were broken out, the tabernacle, the font … everything was missing. Even the cross on the front of the lectern had been removed. You could tell where these things had been placed, but the items themselves were gone. Even the frescoes had been scratched off beyond recognition. All gold leaf had been removed; stolen, most likely. This relieved any anxiety I felt while seeking sanctuary—*irony was a bitch*—in a church. As with the cemetery in Livermore when this odyssey began, I wondered about consecrated ground. Obviously, the plot where this cathedral sat had been befouled and was no longer holy.

"How in the hell … ?"

"That's not important right now. Don't you worry about it."

An empty stone vault sat in the middle of the crypt. It

didn't look very comfortable, but with the way I slept, comfort really didn't matter.

"What about you?"

"Don't worry about me, I'll be fine, and I'll be back for you shortly after sundown, promise."

I made a bed out of what I could find in the interior of the vault and settled in. Dietrich's face was the last thing I saw as he slid the heavy stone cap into place.

CHAPTER IV

I'm not sure how long I was awake before I decided to try to move the vault lid myself. I grew impatient waiting for Dietrich. The inside of the sarcophagus was rough, and the longer I stayed inside, the more uncomfortable and restless I became. There was no coffin, and this concrete vault wasn't the most comfortable thing in the world. Maybe that was a good thing; this way, I didn't feel like I had been buried permanently. I was used to rising shortly after sundown and going about my business, except for that whole getting trapped in the coal mine thing. Details, details.

"Fuck it."

Even for one blessed—or cursed, rather, with preternatural strength, the stone slab was heavy; at least, heavier than I thought it would be. Maybe it was my lack of leverage.

Who knew? What I did know was that I needed out. I needed to stretch my legs and move. With some effort, I finally got it to slide out of the way. The sound of rock grinding on rock reminded me of the ordeal in the coal mine...

... and I shuddered at the thought.

As I sat up, I twisted in my seat to take in my surroundings. Dietrich and I were in a bit of a hurry the night before, so I hadn't had a chance to get the lay of the land, as it were. This dilapidated cathedral wasn't very inviting, and it reminded me of the loft where Andrei had taken me and turned me...

... and I shuddered at the thought.

Dietrich had said he'd be along to collect me after sunset. My sense of time was totally out of whack after spending days in the coal mine with no concept of day or night. I needed to reset my body clock. I surveyed the crypt and had the sinking feeling that I wasn't alone. Detecting warmth and hearing a faint heartbeat, I strained and squinted to see who was there. I may not have spent that much time with the intrepid detective, but I knew what his presence *felt* like. And this wasn't him. In fact, the more I thought about it, I had never really detected heat or a heartbeat when I was with him. Odd. Maybe I was just misremembering. Maybe there were other priorities when I had been with him, and I just wasn't paying attention.

My ability to see in the dark served me well, but I all I could make out was the mirror reflection of what little light there was in a pair of orbs in a cluttered corner. Animal eye shine?

"Blackfoot? Is that you, kitty? Come here, baby."

Nothing. That cat had found her way to impossible places and into implausible spaces. I had no reason to think she couldn't find me here, but my calls went unanswered. I planted my palms on the edges of the vault and pushed myself up and out. Before I could hunt for the mystery presence, I heard shuffling and rustling and the telltale sounds of someone descending rickety wooden steps. This was becoming a recurring theme.

"Elizabeth?"

"Jonas? It's about fucking time."

"I am so sorry. I got jammed up with a case."

Pouting, I said, "But you told me you'd be here right after sunset."

I threw my arms around him in an uncharacteristic display of affection. I was genuinely glad to see him. His signature trench coat was musty but oddly comforting as Dietrich enveloped me. I have only felt comfortable for a short while since Andrei did this to me. Since that assclown turned me into this ... this thing. And that was with Billy. He was such a help to me. He was easy to talk to and did just about anything I asked. We all know how *that* turned out. I warned that little prick not to betray me. Maybe Dietrich could be my new compatriot, my new confidant, my new helper, my protector.

I whispered, "I don't think we're alone."

"Wait ... what?"

"I thought it was my demon cat, but I'm pretty sure there's someone else in here with us. When I pushed my way out of the vault, I sensed someone or *something* in this crypt ... and obviously, it wasn't you."

Dietrich produced a Zippo lighter and put flame to wick on several candles. As the flickering light illuminated the space, I scanned the room again and came up with nothing. Nobody. Not even a rat. My new best friend then opened his coat and produced a blood bag from a San Francisco blood bank and tossed it to me. I popped it open like it was a Capri Sun and sucked it down like I had been frolicking on the beach in SoCal.

Wiping my mouth in a rather unladylike way, I gulped and said, "You know, refrigerated blood only does so much ... only goes so far. Kinda like the rats in the coal mine. They sufficed in a pinch, but there is nothing like hot, living human blood."

"Well, I wasn't about to bring you a fresh victim to feed on. We discussed this in the house at Moss Beach. You've killed a lot of people. I cannot in good conscience feed that habit. I know what you are, and I know what you need to survive. You need to learn how to control this ... this ... thirst."

"But how, Jonas? Seriously. You have no idea what it feels like ... what it does to me."

"I know more than you think, and I understand better than you could ever possibly know."

"But how?"

"I told you. Andrei killed my grandfather. I've been tracking that bastard a long time."

"Find anything interesting in my sketchbook?"

"Huh, wha … ? Oh, yeah. I guess you could say that. It just confirmed what I already knew and what I had surmised."

"I want it back."

"I know."

"Can we get out of here? I don't like it here."

"Of course."

Dietrich offered his arm. We headed up that rickety set of steps to the cathedral. The night air was warm, and the detective's pace was quick as we walked to the familiar Crown Vic. We drove in silence as he guided the car south and then east toward San Francisco. The City. He reached down between my legs…

"Excuse me, Detective!"

He smirked and winked at me as he returned to his upright and proper driving position. There was a small Styrofoam cooler on the floor that I hadn't noticed when I got into the car. Dietrich pulled out another blood bag. This one I sipped.

"Eight pints of blood in the human body. As you pointed out, I don't think two is quite enough for you."

"It's not just the quantity, as I mentioned, it has to be *living* blood. This refrigerated sludge barely gives me any energy."

"I can't exactly let you continue to rampage all over Northern California, now, can I?"

"Well, Columbo, I hope you have a solution, because at this rate, I may just rampage on you," I said with a smirk and winked.

"Well, we wouldn't want that, now, would we? Who's Columbo?"

My hand found my brow and a not so nice snicker escaped my mouth as I shook my head. "I swear, these kids today."

"What? I'm more well-read than you think. I've been told I have an old soul."

"That may be, but your pop culture history knowledge is shit."

"Well, I am only twenty-six. Seriously, who's Columbo?"

"Never mind, Sherlock."

"Ah, that one I get."

Dietrich pressed the gas pedal a little harder and set his jaw as we made our way into The City. Before long, we were seated in a booth at a Starbucks. I must've been a sight after what I had just been through. The Starbucks may have been one I'd popped into; it may have been one I'd visited with Julie. My memory was fuzzy. Everything from that time was a blur. From those first few days after escaping from the morgue to the rail yard and eventually the coal mine, the past several weeks had flown by. The revelations about Andrei and Dietrich had been mind-blowing, to say the least. My thoughts often returned to the boutique in Livermore and my parents.

"I have something to tell you, Elizabeth."

Dietrich's voice broke my concentration as I was reflecting on the past few months while he ordered coffee I wasn't going to drink. Appearances, you know?

"Hold that thought."

I excused myself and went to the restroom to try to do something with my appearance. There were times when I really didn't give a shit about not casting a reflection, and there were others when it was a real pain in the ass. This was one of the latter. After a quick scrub and an attempt at dusting myself off, I returned to the detective.

"You were saying'?" I asked, looking at him and his trench coat sitting across from me.

"Well, you know how you were trapped in the coal mine?"

"Yeah?"

"Have you wondered how the cave-in happened?"

"I just figured it was the bumbling SWAT guys who couldn't find me in the tunnels. Figured one of them must've knocked that boulder loose."

"I did it."

"What? *Are you fucking kidding me?*"

I reached across the table and grabbed him by the lapels and pulled him out of his seat. We were nose to nose.

"Why the fuck would you do something that goddamn crazy? You could have killed me."

"I did it to protect you."

"Are you fucking kidding me? Are you out of your fucking mind?"

"Liz ... listen ... "

I relaxed and let go of his coat. We both sat back. I wasn't sure if I really wanted to hear what he had to say.

"By closing the mine, I gave them no reason to keep searching there. They were convinced you were finished."

"Yeah? How the hell would they know that?"

"Why do you think it took me so long to come back for you? I went round and round with the SWAT commander, Tim, and the captain to convince them there was no way you could've survived that cave-in."

"You had no idea where I was in that mine. I could've been crushed."

"It was a chance I had to take."

"Next time, gamble with your own fucking life."

I had really been hoping Jonas was someone I could trust ... someone I could rely on, but this new information troubled me. That was some calculated risk he took with my well-being. It seemed like he genuinely wanted to help. It seemed like he knew an awful lot about what was going on. There was a comfort level I'd felt with him ever since I'd first heard him speak. But there was something else, something I couldn't quite put my finger on. My predatory instincts didn't kick in when I was with him. I normally picked up heat and heartbeats when I needed to feed. But when I was with Dietrich, I didn't read much of anything. This troubled me.

"Come on, let's go for a walk," Dietrich said as he grabbed my hand and practically dragged me out of my seat in the booth. With the opposite hand, he pushed the door open and we breezed into the night. Although the Powell Street location was open twenty-four hours, I couldn't imagine sitting and talking all night without actually, you know, drinking coffee. I really hadn't been paying attention during the drive from Pacifica, but now I was fully aware of where I was. The coffee shop was on the corner of Powell and O'Farrell. Ridiculously close to The Dark Truth, and a lot of other ... things.

I grabbed Dietrich by the sleeve and tugged him in the other direction. The Dark Truth and that parking garage were the last places I wanted to go. And I was getting thirsty. I needed to move on from the night that I was kidnapped and where it had happened. I needed to find a new hunting ground. I needed to reevaluate my look. I needed a lot of things.

What I didn't need was a chaperone. Billy had been a great compatriot. We had grown to enjoy each other's company, and he'd appreciated what I was, even if he hadn't really understood it. He'd learned his place in the relationship. His betrayal still stung, and I didn't regret dispatching him and his family, not one bit. But I didn't know what to make of Dietrich. It was almost as if he were trying to keep an eye on me to prevent me from hunting.

It was funny. I had spent so much time trying to get to Dietrich to learn what he knew and discern how close the authorities were to solving the mysteries that Andrei and I were creating all over Northern California. Now I had him, and I didn't know what to do with him.

What I did know was that we needed to walk in the opposite direction. I also knew that I needed to shake him so I could hunt. Dietrich finally got the hint after quite a bit of insistent tugging and the childlike pleading look on my face. He reluctantly tagged along. Good thing, too. I thought I was going to pull his arm out of the socket.

We walked along O'Farrell and headed toward Market Street. Third Street loomed ahead. Damned if we did, damned if we didn't. In one direction was where this macabre adventure began, and in the other, a whole bunch of other craziness I didn't want to think about. But this vector offered far fewer traumatic memories. We ended up at Local Edition, a newspaper-themed bar. Of course we did.

There was something about this old soul with whom I was spending the evening. Something *old*, all right. He may have said he was twenty-six; his online exploits may have told a story about a young, hotshot detective who had vaulted up the ranks impossibly fast, but my skepticism was on the rise. My woman's intuition was in full effect, and I was thankful it hadn't died when I did. From the dusty case files to the haunts he frequented, there was something mysterious about my companion, and I was determined to find it.

Did I mention I was getting thirsty?

Dietrich had this vibe ... this air about him. It was almost like he had stepped out of a classic film noir, except he was just missing the fedora. As easily as he moved through night, he didn't quite seem to *belong*. He would have been at home alongside Robert Mitchum in *Out of the Past,* or opposite Ann Savage in *Detour,* so it was no surprise that he had picked this spot for us to stay a while.

We were greeted almost immediately.

"Waddaya say, Joe?"

"Jonas," the maitre d' deadpanned as he threw a disapproving glance in my direction.

"Is my booth available?"

"It is." Joe turned on a heel and led us to a table in the back corner. This was becoming a theme with Dietrich. "I'll send Christina over."

"Thanks, Joe."

The well-dressed, well-appointed maitre d' strolled to the bar, leaned over, and engaged in a hushed conversation with a person I could only assume was Christina. An attractive, well-groomed woman in her early thirties looked in our direction and nodded as Joe spoke. She cleaned rocks glasses without pause as Joe went on. I didn't like it when people talked about me behind my back, and I certainly didn't care for it happening in front of my face.

Dietrich noticed that my comfort level had shifted with my observation. Rather than stare at the folks talking about me, I took in the joint. It was certainly more upscale than I would've anticipated. I was thankful that tonight was not a night for live music. The piped-in tunes were straight out of the 1940s.

"I love this spot," Dietrich said with a smile and a note of glee.

"I can see why. There is definitely more to you, Detective. There is so much you display outwardly, but you're like an iceberg. I think most of you exists beneath this facade." I chose the last word very carefully.

I pretended to peruse the menu as Dietrich studied my face. Christina finally made her way over. She was professional; cordial, but when it came to my companion, familiar. Maybe too familiar. Her hair was pulled back into a tight ponytail. Her tight, crisp white blouse had an extra button undone and complemented her form-fitting black slacks. She had dazzling, intense blue eyes and supple lips, and she was particularly voluptuous.

She arched one eyebrow as she ignored me and greeted Dietrich. "Evening, Jonas. Usual?"

"Of course."

"And for your friend?"

"I'll have—" Dietrich cut me off.

"Same."

"You got it. Two Bloody Marys coming right up."

He had to know I wasn't going to touch mine. But I

guess keeping up appearances was necessary if I was going to mix and mingle with the populace. Considering that other than my brief stint in the bathroom at Starbucks, I hadn't had a chance to clean up or even freshen up after my ... ordeal, I was sure I was quite the sight.

The ever-deepening mystery that was Detective Sergeant Jonas Dietrich was starting to become maddening. There was so much more to him than he let on. The loner, the outcast, the lone wolf ... he certainly seemed to have connections and relationships with folks all over the San Francisco Bay Area. And nighttime seemed to suit him very well.

Christina was quick to bring our drinks.

"Thanks, Chris."

"Uh-huh."

"Did the temperature drop in here, or is it just me?" I asked after our server was out of earshot.

"Whatever do you mean?"

"Uh-huh."

He obviously had history with Christina and this joint. I wouldn't exactly call it animosity, but it wasn't exactly warmth, either. He may have been the detective, but I was determined to get to the bottom of who he was. However, I had this sinking feeling it wasn't going to be tonight, or anytime soon, for that matter. The thirst had me. Four pints of donated blood sucked out of plastic bags in the past twenty-four hours or so just didn't cut it. He had to know that, didn't he? He knew so much about vampires. He had to know that. Didn't he?

It was a slow night at Local Edition. Must have been a weeknight. I was still getting my body clock in order. Most of the folks that came in didn't have reservations and just found their way to the bar or a bistro table or booth. Food wasn't exactly churning out from the kitchen, but the booze was certainly flowing from the bar. The noise level varied as patrons came and went. I really wasn't paying much attention.

The thirst.

"Would you excuse me, please?"

"Of course. Are you all right?"

"Yeah, I just need to … um … freshen up."

"It's right through there," Dietrich said as he motioned toward the restrooms.

Dietrich was stunned when I leaned over and kissed him on the cheek as I rose to my feet. I whispered in his ear, "I want my sketchbook." He responded with an audible gulp.

I smoothed myself over after my spontaneous display of affection and headed toward the ladies' room. The appointments in this place were truly spectacular, from the antique typewriters to the encased editions of old newspaper front pages. The proprietors had really thought of everything. I couldn't be bothered with all that. Maybe in another life I could have enjoyed this spot, but not now. Not tonight.

The corridor to the restroom was surprisingly narrow. The entry to the kitchen was at the end past the doors to the men's and ladies' facilities. I also had to walk past the bar and servers' station to get there. I saw Christina breaking down cardboard boxes after restocking some bottled beer.

I slipped into the kitchen as quickly and as quietly as possible. The short-order cooks were too busy to notice a civilian in their midst. I scanned the room, searching for the back entrance, and headed for it as soon as I spotted it. I had a plan. It wasn't much of a plan, but it was still a plan. I slipped out the back entrance and found what I was seeking: the loading dock and trash area. A large recycling bin sat next to a large metal dumpster. I shimmied between them and crouched down.

Two busboys exited the bar carrying empty boxes and trash bags, but I didn't want them. I made myself as small as possible and hid from view as they deposited their refuse in the bins. They chatted boisterously as they completed their task and went back to the kitchen.

Did I mistime my hunt? Did I misjudge my quarry?

Thankfully, I didn't have to wait long.

After emerging from the kitchen and stepping into the alley, Christina dropped her empty beer cases and retreated when she saw me spring from the darkness. Although I hadn't hunted in several days, I didn't miss a beat. The instincts came flooding back. After pouncing on her and tackling her to the ground, I covered Christina's mouth with my left hand and restrained her with my knees. All my weight drove down on her biceps, giving me leverage and preventing her from grabbing me. She thrust her hips and thrashed her legs in a vain effort to toss me off.

"Scream, and you die. Blink twice if you understand."

It took her a few seconds to realize that she had been asked a question and a response was required. She blinked twice, and I removed my hand from her mouth. I stared deep into her sizzling blue eyes. Her pupils, already wide from the lack of light, dilated to an impossible diameter. I grabbed her by the wrists and pinned them over her head while I slid my body down on top of hers, my knees coming to rest alongside her hips.

There was something about Christina from the moment I saw her. It may have been her attitude, how aloof and disaffected she was, how frosty she was, or maybe I just liked her eyes.

I slipped my right hand behind her head and removed the rubber band securing her ponytail. I balled her hair into a fist and yanked her head back. My left hand took control of both her wrists and kept her pinned. My tongue found her skin in the unbuttoned top of her blouse and I licked her from her cleavage to the tip of her nose. She was sweating. Tiny, salty drops of perspiration bubbled on top of gooseflesh. She shuddered in fear. Goosebumps erupted along her throat as I grazed her skin. Her jugular pulsed with blood. I was aroused. I think she was, too. My sex throbbed as I kissed her full on the mouth. My hungry tongue found hers. The thirst was building. The thirst was blinding.

I broke the kiss with a gasp. Her hips rose to meet my inner thighs. I ripped her blouse open. I reared my head back as a hiss escaped my throat and bared my fangs. The look of wanton desire on Christina's face was replaced by sheer terror. I dropped my full weight on her and forced her left breast out of her bra with my teeth. Her breast filled my mouth and my tongue found her nipple. She groaned with pleasure and writhed under me. My fangs pierced her nipple and loosed the blood. I suckled as the blood squirted into my mouth.

Frustration set in quickly as the blood simply did not flow fast enough. My lower lip dragged across Christina's flesh to her throat. I traced her jugular with my tongue until I found a sweet spot. My fangs pierced her flesh with little effort. When the vein wall broke and released a torrent of blood, it drove me over the edge. My orgasm struck like lightning when the sweet crimson nectar hit my taste buds. My knees clenched and squeezed her pulsing oblique muscles.

I loosened my grip on her hair and let go of her wrists as her body let go of her life. Christina's heart, the heart that had thumped with inexplicable passion moments earlier, slowed and eventually stopped. I rocked back on my heels as I relaxed.

Christina's body was lifeless beneath me, as cold as the asphalt I pinned her to. The light in her blazing blue eyes had dimmed and her tongue lolled out of her mouth ... the mouth I'd graced with my first same-sex kiss. The thought had never occurred to me before then. I was strangely attracted to Christina and didn't know why. I had never been attracted to females before. I wasn't even one of those girls who "experimented" in college.

I basked in the afterglow of having slaked my unnatural thirst and the most amazing climax ever. As much as I would have liked to revel in it, my time was up. And now was certainly not the time for an introspective examination of my sexual preferences.

The sound of Dietrich bursting through the exit to the loading dock snapped me out of my ecstasy. He was neither slow nor graceful, and he was aghast when he saw what I had done. The look on his face confirmed my earlier suspicions about a history between him and Christina. It dawned on me that maybe she had been cold to us when she took our order because she was jealous. For all my preternatural abilities and senses, I could be pretty dense.

I rose to my full height, Christina's blood running down my chin and neck to my décolletage.

"Elizabeth!" Dietrich shouted. "Oh, my God! What have you done? No, no, NO."

The shock and alarm quickly became a scolding. I was not about to be admonished by a veritable child. I said nothing. An animal growl emanated from my throat. I felt it before I heard it. It was a sound I didn't know I was capable of making, and I kind of liked it.

I quickly scanned the alley, assessing my options for an acceptable escape route. I spotted a shape at one end. A human shape. Andrei? It couldn't have been. The build was all wrong. The stance was all wrong. This figure was tall, hulking, menacing. Andrei was a lot of things, but he was none of those. I took off running in the opposite direction.

No one pursued; no one chased; no one called into the blackness.

CHAPTER V

Slinking and scuttling, skulking and stealing my way, I traversed the alleys from Market to Folsom. I dodged busboys and bartenders as they made their trash runs. One unfortunate soul was unable to press himself to a wall fast enough. My shoulder met him flush in the sternum and sent him flying. I didn't even stop to help him up and just blew past him.

I turned right on Folsom and slowed to a fast walk as I crossed 3rd Street and then to a normal pace as I crossed 4th. By the time I got to 5th, it had started raining. It wasn't gradual. It didn't start as a mist. It was an instant drizzle. I instinctively wrapped my arms around my torso as my pace slowed.

My purposeful walking became aimless wandering. My mind went blank as I started counting my footsteps. I got past one hundred before I realized what I was doing. I smashed my palm into my forehead repeatedly to drive the impulse away.

If I could have cried I would have been bawling. Instead, my chest rose and fell, and I convulsed with dry, airless heaves. I finally took stock of my situation. Here I was, wandering the streets of San Francisco again, with nowhere to go, no money, no transportation, no destination, no sanctuary. I'd just burned my only friend. No hope.

My parents were dead. Billy, my human concierge, was dead. Julie, my best friend and confidant, was dead. Andrei was … well, he was supposed to be dead. Dietrich … God, what the fuck was my problem when it came to him? I'd left him in an alley after I had worked so hard to get back to him, and after he went through all that trouble to rescue me.

What was Dietrich's deal anyway? Why was I drawn to him? Why did I find him attractive? I did, didn't I? And what the fuck was going on with me when I'd killed Christina? What was it about her? She was beautiful, but in a girl-next-door kind of way. But her eyes … oh, those azure pools.

I had never been attracted to women in my natural born life. Not even Julie. I had moments after the … turning when I wanted her, but not like that. I wanted her blood. Not her body. But Christina. I'd wanted to consume Christina. That was the only way to describe it. The kill would've been satisfying unto itself. I hadn't fed in God knows how long, and Dietrich thought a couple of bags of blood from the International House of Plasma would be enough to suffice. Suffice until when?

What the hell did Dietrich know, and how did he know it? And why couldn't I *read* him? What did he find in my sketchbook? How was I going to get it back?

I had kinda blown that, hadn't I?

I turned the questions over and over and dumped them into the blender in my mind, hoping to come up with some answers. As frustrating as it was not to be able to answer them, it was better than counting. Before I knew it, I had crossed 10th. I turned right on 11th and headed back toward Market Street.

Dietrich was the key. If I hadn't been convinced before, I was now. I'm pretty sure he was the detective that was there the night they found me naked, murdered, crucified, and drained of blood. I'd followed him back to the abandoned loft where I'd lost my life. The conversation I'd overheard between him and his colleague, Tim, was very telling. Tim had turned out to be quite the pain in the ass, but that wasn't important right now. The conversation Dietrich and I'd had at Tunnel Top … that could have been something, but we'd been so rudely interrupted. Then the rising of the giant orange ball of fusion reactor in the sky prevented the chat at Moss Beach from being productive. We hadn't had any time to talk prior to the knock-down, drag-out with Andrei. And we all knew how tonight had worked out.

Here's what I knew, or thought I knew, about Dietrich. He was a young hotshot in the San Francisco Police Department. He had risen up the ranks quickly, but was ostracized. He was allowed to work odd cases solo on the fringe. He seemed to only surface at night. He had a penchant for frequenting some strange places. He was old school; a gumshoe; dusty, musty, scholarly, bookish.

And he had my sketchbook.

I quickened my pace as a new idea struck me. The rain worsened as I broke right on Market and headed back toward Local Edition. Maybe Dietrich was still there. I wondered if he had called for backup, or if anyone had called the cops after what I'd done to Christina. I was really starting to wonder about that shadowy figure in the alley.

As I crossed Ellis and 4th along Market, I could see the lights from various emergency vehicles. Fuck. Dietrich had called in the cavalry. I walked, slowing down as I got closer. Just as I passed a 7-11, someone grabbed me and pulled me off the sidewalk. A hand covered my mouth.

"Shhh … "

I recognized the trench coat sleeves. Never mind who it was; getting waylaid like this was becoming tiresome.

"I'm going to take my hand away, but you need to be quiet. Do you understand?"

I nodded rapidly and nervously. Why didn't I feel warmth from his hand? Dietrich released me. I spun to confront him. He wore the trench coat over the gray wool suit he'd worn earlier and had added a gangster fedora. And he was drenched.

"What the fuck, Jonas?"

"I could ask you the same question. What the hell did you do to Christina? And why?"

"I wish I knew. I don't know myself."

"Well, you've gotten us into quite the mess."

"Did you call for backup?"

"No. One of the busboys found her. Luckily, he didn't see me."

"What about the other guy?"

"What other guy?"

"I saw someone at the other end of the alley. At first, I thought it might have been Andrei, but he was too big. Different."

"I didn't see anyone. Look, I need to get back there. I don't think Joe is going to be too sympathetic. He's very well aware that Christina and I had a thing once."

"How did I know? It wasn't obvious or anything. As much as you try to be this shadowy figure, you aren't very subtle."

"I hope that's not why you did what you did."

"Don't flatter yourself, detective. I was thirsty, and some of that was your fault. Cold blood bags. Four pints, my ass."

He handed me a burner cell phone.

"Here, I'll get in touch later. We'll figure out where to put you for the rest of the night, but I have to go help clean up this mess first."

"Put me? Really? Ass."

He left me in the downpour. I watched as his hat and coat got smaller and smaller as he made his way along

Market to Local Edition. I waited until his silhouette was among his brethren before I followed. I stacked a couple pallets and scrambled to the rooftop of a nearby one-story building.

While I watched the emergency personnel bustle about with their various tasks ... taking photos, gathering evidence, cordoning off the area, interviewing witnesses, preparing to remove the body, etc. ... my thoughts wandered to Dietrich. That sliver was back in my brain. You know that itch deep in your psyche you can't reach? I thought about how he'd extracted me from the coal mine and what he must have endured while trying to explain himself to his superiors and fellow cops.

The activity that unfolded before me was eerily similar to what Billy and I had witnessed that night we'd tried to get Andrei pinched. The emergency lights, the black and whites, the ambulance, uniformed cops canvassing the area and interviewing witnesses. The scene was becoming all too familiar. From the night my body was discovered or when the cops rousted us from Julie's apartment, to the night in the abandoned warehouse where Andrei was almost apprehended and two high-spirited encounters with the SFPD SWAT team, I was becoming way too familiar with the procedures of the local authorities. Hell, I should probably be on a first-name basis with some of these first responders by now.

I tried to keep an eye on my intrepid detective as he weaved his way through the maze of hustle and bustle behind Local Edition. My thirst, my need to hunt, and my momentary infatuation with Christina had created a giant mess. This might end up being my most high-profile kill yet, and I'd had some doozies.

My reminiscing was distracting me from observing my on-again, off-again partner. Actually, I wasn't sure what he was to me. The whole thing was so fucking confusing and frustrating. I was drawn to him, but I also felt the overwhelming urge to get away from him, to do my own thing and find my own way. On the other hand, I felt the most secure when I had a human companion to keep watch during the day and help me navigate the night.

But I was a creature of the night. A denizen of the night. What goes bump in the night. Self-sufficiency was going to be key for me to survive. I had already made my peace with what I was. Dispatching the traitorous Billy and his family had been the final nudge down the slippery slope to oblivion. It had steeled my nerves for my confrontation with Andrei at Sutro Baths and helped me shed the last vestiges of my humanity.

Now I was whining and pining for a human companion, a confederate … what was the word witches used? Familiar? But Dietrich didn't fit that mold. He wasn't young and pliable like Billy; he wasn't middle-aged and pliable like Julie. That was just it. I didn't know what the fuck he was. Every human I'd encountered since that night and since my "awakening" in that morgue drawer had emitted a signature. I could read their body heat, I could sense their heartbeat, and I could even gauge their fear. But Dietrich? Well, that was the conundrum, wasn't it? He didn't emit a signature. The only other entity I had experienced this with had been Andrei. Just like Dietrich, he had been arresting; captivating, even if it had been in a bad way.

I shook it off. The thought that crept in my head was too much to bear. Of course, I was distracted when I was in their respective presences. When it had been Andrei, I was afraid, apprehensive; I was in awe of my "maker." I shuddered to even think that of him. I was also incensed when I was in his presence. With Dietrich it was the same, but different. I wasn't concerned with him as possible prey, nor did I fear him. I was intrigued when I was with him. He captivated me. He had knowledge I wanted … no, needed.

That's what it was. I didn't think of him as game. He wasn't a prey animal … well, not in the "I need to drain every drop of his blood" kind of way. More like in an Indiana Jones archaeology kind of way. Yeah, that' was it.

The warm summer drizzle was now a shower, and it soaked to the bone. The water cleansed the air. It dripped from my brow to my eyelashes and onto my cheeks. The drops blurred my vision as I tried to keep up with the action behind the bar where I had claimed Christina's life.

The first responders and emergency vehicles started to disperse. I watched in wistful remembrance as a couple of EMTs loaded her exquisite body into the ambulance and drove away. I could just make out her shape under the crisp, white sheet. My right eyebrow raised, I licked my lips and made a "yummy" sound as I thought I saw a bloodstain spreading through the fabric.

Dietrich finally emerged from the circus of activity, jotting notes in his little detective notebook, shaking hands with colleagues, pausing to take a quick phone call … you know, cop shit. As he left the alley and started back toward the convenience store where he'd left me, he glanced up. I smiled when my eyes met his. He did not return the gesture. Instead, he flashed me a look of confusion that became consternation followed yet again by horror.

CHAPTER VI

The clouds had parted enough to let some moonlight through. The burner phone Dietrich had slipped me sprang to life with a shrill, annoying melody. I flipped it open. A reflection in the view screen caught my attention before I could raise the device to my ear. A shadow galvanized me into action. I spun around to find a large man hulking over me, his arm raised high in the air, and what looked to be, *no … it couldn't be*, a sharp wooden stake clutched in his meaty fist, poised to strike. I crouched down and hissed like a cat just as he swung the stake and missed. My fangs were bared. I deftly avoided what was meant to be a killing blow, one I was not meant to see coming.

A large crucifix on a chain around my assailant's neck swung into view. My eyes burned at the sight of it. My skin crawled. It was a sensation I had never experienced before, not even when I was human; not even when I realized Andrei had been stalking me all these years.

My attacker was huge. Six foot four, two hundred and eighty pounds if I had to hazard a guess. He had long, wet hair that framed a deeply lined, weathered face, a face that had seen his dark robe-clad *(robe? Who the fuck wears a robe?)* body do unspeakable things.

I had nowhere to go. He had me cornered on the roof of this building. I felt stupid for leaving myself exposed like this. For some I reason, I had not felt like I had any natural predators. I'd never thought I might have some unnatural ones. He regained his composure after missing his sure strike and started in on me. I retreated until I felt the backs of my legs hit the edge of the roof.

He inched closer and closer. He had malice in his eyes. Hate. Contempt. Indignation. Yet no fear.

That fucking cross again.

I tumbled over.

My body struggled to right itself as I fell all of one story to the sidewalk below. I would have made an Olympic gymnast proud as I stuck the landing. Just as my feet hit and my left knee dropped to the ground, my hands reached for concrete. Before I could stand up, someone tossed a tarp over me, and I was whisked down the street, away from Local Edition and the WWE's resident vampire slayer. Moving southwest along Market, I recognized that my savior was familiar. In less than a block, I realized that the protective tarp that had been thrown around me was in fact

Dietrich's God-awful trench coat. He was frantically searching for somewhere for us to put in as we tried to put distance between us and my stake-wielding new friend.

"Would you please get off me?"

"No, not yet; not until we're safe."

"I'm a big girl. I can take care of myself."

"Right, that's why you almost got killed tonight."

"Well, that's not important right now."

"You're right, it's not. We'll discuss that later. Right now, we need to get the fuck out of here."

We crossed Market at 4th and doubled back to Geary Street via Stockton. Before long, we were back at the Crown Vic. Dietrich jammed the key in the ignition and, as he turned it, the engine roared to life. He slammed the column shifter into gear and tromped on the gas. Tires squealed and smoked as he laid down rubber on the wet pavement as we sped away.

There was no sign of my attacker.

The ride to the abandoned cathedral was mercifully short. I wasn't sure why Dietrich was fixated on the place. Maybe he knew it was safe. Maybe he had attended services there when he was a kid, or in another life. Maybe there was another reason, one woven into the fabric of the mystery that was Jonas Dietrich. It might not happen this night or the next, but I was going to find out about this guy, dammit. Every time I'd tried to distance myself from him, I found myself right back with him.

Funny. I'd tried to do the same thing with Julie, and we

all know how that had turned out. I wasn't about to let my nocturnal proclivities get Jonas killed. Andrei was still out there somewhere, more than likely, and now I had a new enemy. I hadn't nearly ended up on the wrong end of a sharp wooden stake by accident. This guy knew what I was, and I was what he was after. That was an unsettling thought. Not once did I think that Andrei was the only vampire on the planet, nor did I believe there was an underground vampire cabal with shadow governments and private armies. But the thought of actual vampire hunters in this world—assassins trained to do battle with the undead—had never occurred to me. Not even once.

After all the horror movies I had watched growing up and all the books I had read, my turning had been a singular experience. I had been so caught up in the events of the past few months, so immersed in becoming the "new" me, that I had forgotten to tap into the knowledge base in my brain. During all those blocks I walked, the miles I drove or rode, I never pondered the implications my existence might have for the world, only how it affected *me*. How shortsighted and selfish of me. Even when I was thinking of others, it seemed to backfire. Damned if I did, damned if I didn't.

Whenever I sought a confidant or a confederate, I was afraid that person would end up getting hurt, or worse. Whenever I distanced myself from that ally, they ended up dead. Julie was Andrei's doing. Had I stayed with her, maybe I could have protected her. Billy, on the other hand ... well,

Billy was a different story altogether, wasn't he? The boy had been enamored by the vampire culture. Why wasn't he enamored by me? Obviously, my threats weren't enough to dissuade him from betraying me. Neither was the relationship we'd forged. Heavy-handed, I know, but I'd thought Billy and I had developed a real bond on the way to a mutually beneficial symbiotic relationship. Guess I'd been wrong, and he'd paid for his mistake with his own life and his family's lives. I'd warned him.

What the fuck did I know? Seriously.

CHAPTER VII

Dietrich found a spot two blocks from the dilapidated church, threw the shifter into park, and cut the engine. We walked in silence, stealthily let ourselves back into the church, and went down to the crypt. I sheepishly handed the coat to Dietrich like a jilted high school girl giving the star quarterback his letterman' jacket back.

"His name is Serge."

This statement was delivered in a matter-of-fact, emotionless monotone. I was stunned. My jaw dropped. My heart sank. My stomach turned. I tried to respond but I all I could manage was a stammer.

"He is a church-trained vampire hunter."

"Ya think?" I was incredulous. I couldn't believe my ears. I knew Dietrich was into some dark shit, especially considering his extensive research and detective work on

Andrei, but this? This was a bombshell, and I was shell-shocked. In the span of a few hours, I had gone from my most public and ill-advised impulsive kill to date to discovering that there were such things as vampire slayers and that Dietrich fucking knew all this and hadn't seen fit to say a goddamn word about it.

"And not for one instant did you think this information was pertinent?"

"It never came up. I was meaning to say something. I was going to tell you tonight, actually, but you decided to dine on Christina before I had a chance."

"That's awfully convenient, Jonas. There was history between you two, wasn't there? Why in the hell did you take me to that place?"

"I thought she'd quit."

"Well, you thought wrong, didn't you?"

"You confirmed one thing, though."

"Oh, and what was that?"

"You found her as … appetizing … as I did."

"Ugh! What the hell is that supposed to mean? Never mind. I don't want to know. I thought you were different, Jonas, I really did."

And I did; I still did. I just didn't know *what* made him different. There was something there, something that itched and ached, and it wasn't entirely unpleasant. But this revelation was startling, and I needed to get to the bottom of a few things before I went diving into Dietrich's backstory.

"Okay, spill it. Who the fuck is this 'Serge,' or whatever you said his name was?"

"I'll tell you what I know. Cop a squat."

"How sophisticated."

We each found something to sit on, nothing too comfortable, but we made do. I sat cross-legged while he manspread and took up enough space for three of him. The sight drew a huff from me.

"Serge Da Rocha. Like I said, church-trained—"

"Brazilian?"

"Portuguese."

"Which church?"

"All of them."

"What the fuck do you mean, all of them?"

"Exactly what I said. All of them. He has studied vampirism in every major faith and religion on this planet. Islam, Judaism, Buddhism, Hinduism, Shao Lin, Ancient Egyptian, Catholicism, Protestantism, Eastern Orthodox … Greek Orthodox. And he has dispatched every species of vampire—"

"How the hell—"

"Every culture, well, *almost* every culture has a vampire myth, legend, or folklore. When a local parish, synagogue, mosque, temple, or what-have-you discovers or believes that they have a vampire infestation on their hands, they get in touch with Da Rocha through the affected parish or what-have-you. He has battled the lidéric in Hungary; the rakshasas of India; kappas in Japan; lampirs and vjesci, and the Dearg-Dul of Ireland, among others in Europe; and vrykolakas. That's what you are ... more than likely."

"Infestation? Like I'm some kind of vermin?"

"To them, that's exactly what you are. A scourge, a virus, an invasive species; something that needs to be stamped out, lest your evil—"

"Evil? And who are *them*?"

"Their word, not mine ... lest your evil spreads and infects the local parishioners. He is the most skilled and accomplished slayer I have ever ... "

His voice trailed off, and I could tell he was reluctant to finish that sentence. He knew more than he was telling, and I wasn't sure if I should press him on it just yet. I didn't get the chance, because Dietrich had just dropped another bombshell on me. It was an admission I kinda saw coming, but it was a shock to my system nonetheless. Since Detective Sergeant Jonas Dietrich had come into my life, I had often wondered about his routine, his dynamic with his superiors, and his caseload. He seemed to work only at night. He worked the odd cases, the ones no one else wanted. He had this *X-Files*/Fox Mulder, *Se7en*/Detective Mills thing going on. He was a loner, an outcast, an outsider.

He had carte blanche to work these cases in the shadows.

But this. This was different. I had put him in an untenable situation. Well, to be honest, he'd started it. Did he really think a couple bags from the local blood bank would be enough to slake my thirst? My time in the coal mine was reminiscent of the night I'd missed a feeding, which had led to that hell I'd created in the boutique in Livermore. The thirst had morphed into a hunger. A gnawing. A clawing at my innards. A couple of pints slurped from plastic bags were far from satisfying.

To be fair, I could have done better to control myself with Christina. But there was something about her ... something I couldn't put a finger on, so I put my mouth on her instead. Although taking her blood ... her life ... had been an intense, almost existential experience, Dietrich was now compromised professionally and personally. I was clueless about exactly how compromised.

"I have to go."

"Somehow I knew you were going to say that. It's my fault. I'm sorry."

"Yeah, well, this is going to be impossible to explain. Serge's appearance allowed me to slip away before I was forced to answer for what you did to Christina. But I know too many people at Local Edition, and Joe ... well, Joe knows I was there with you. And the kitchen staff knows, too; they saw you leave ... "

"Look, I get it. I just wish we had more time to discuss Serge and his vocation."

"For that, I'm sorry. I think your brazen feeding habits put you on his radar. Vampires such as Andrei have kept a low profile and stayed out of the newspapers, but you ... you're a different animal."

"What am I supposed to do about this guy?"

"Watch your back, keep your head on a swivel, and be diligent."

"Could you sound less like a fucking cop?"

"I need to go."

With a twirl of his trench coat, Dietrich was gone. I reclined in my vault and tried to get a handle on my situation and be sympathetic to his. Dietrich's presence was replaced in short order by Blackfoot's. For the life of me, I did not understand how the damn cat kept finding me. I wasn't even going to complain, though. I was happy for the company. In addition to my unexpected feline bunkmate, I noticed some other critters had taken up residence in the crypt. Mexican free-tailed bats, spiders of untold species, mice, rats, and even an opossum had decided to join me for my daytime slumber. I could almost *hear* them, could almost sense their thoughts. There was an odd comfort in their presence; a strange connection.

There was some time before sunrise, and I had too much on my mind to be able to rest at the moment. Dietrich had been pursuing Andrei for some time, so he undoubtedly had come across quite a bit of information, anecdotal evidence, and whatnot. But I got the impression he'd barely scratched the surface of what he knew when he gave me his *Reader's Digest* version of Serge's biography. I wondered how he knew so much about this rampaging vampire killer, let alone the lore of the undead.

I was falling into a rabbit hole I had no time for at the moment. I could not wrap my head around the possibility of numerous species of vampires roaming the countryside, terrorizing the unsuspecting. How much was real and how much was myth and folklore? Jonas had rattled off several varieties.

My thoughts wandered back to Dietrich and his current predicament, the quandary in which he was now embroiled. I rehashed the events of the evening. As I mentally retraced my steps, the only thing I could come up with was that Dietrich was now a fugitive as well. How could he not be? At best he was an accessory, at worst he was the murderer. I had left him at the table by himself when I pursued Christina. But who would believe that he was not complicit in his ex-girlfriend's murder? I had accompanied him. People saw us together. There was no way he was going to be able to wriggle his way out of the consequences attached to the company he had decided to keep. My tussle with Serge had enabled Dietrich to excuse himself from *my* crime scene. Now I knew why he'd kept the police radio in the Crown Vic switched off on the ride to the cathedral. And why couldn't I read him? Why didn't he register as *prey*?

Fuck.

For the first time since the becoming, I drifted off instead of shut off.

CHAPTER VIII

I woke at sunset refreshed yet confused. My crypt mates had returned. Hell, I thought they might have multiplied. Of course, Blackfoot scampered off the second I moved the slab and rose from the vault. God only knows when I'd see that damn cat again. I was used to her coming and going as she pleased. She had been like that from the beginning, but now it seemed she actually cared for me, although she'd stopped bringing me half-dead vermin she thought I'd enjoy. And I had saved her from the gang of raccoons.

I removed myself from the stone enclosure I now called a bed and wandered around what now sufficed as an apartment. I leaned against the edge of the vault as I surveyed my surroundings. A black widow spider ambled from the stone to my hand and up my arm. In my other life, I would have panicked and probably squished her. Now, I watched with intrigue as her eight legs carried her bulbous body with its red hourglass along my forearm from my elbow. I wasn't afraid. She seemed equally intrigued by me.

I inspected the arachnid with laser focus as she crawled to the back of my hand. Each part of her anatomy revealed itself to me. I counted the segments of each leg, then studied her fangs and spinnerets and her jaws. The harder I concentrated, the more I experienced her. Her legs thundered on my skin like the impact tremors of an elephant. Her jaws and fangs scraped together like blades across a sharpener.

Raising my hand, I brought the spider to my face. I found her tiny eyes. In my mind, I wished her away; I willed her to leave. After a long moment of silence and stillness, the spider ziplined from my hand on a silk thread and crawled into a crevice. *Wait, what?*

After finally turning my attention away from the spider, I regarded the other inhabitants of the crypt. Rats, mice, bats, insects, many species of spider. They all seemed enthralled by me. It was more than animal curiosity. It wasn't predatory behavior; it was respect. Several creepy crawlies slinked, crawled, and scuttled … not toward me, but to me. Blackfoot reappeared out of nowhere and hurled herself against my legs, purring loudly. She wasn't bothered by the other critters, not one bit. On the contrary. The new denizens of the crypt revered the cat and showed her some measure of respect.

Rats and mice stood on their hind legs and sniffed the air. Insects formed a semicircle a few feet in front of me. Spiders clambered over the rubble of the sarcophagi. A vampire bat perched on my shoulder. "A bit out of your range, aren't you, pal?" I regarded him. He was a shaky, twitchy thing, and he allowed me to gently scratch his head between his disproportionately large ears. I could feel him relax as he leaned into my affections.

I gently grabbed the bat, placed him on a marble slab, and stood up. I felt tall. I felt powerful. I felt like a macabre, undead Snow White. I lorded over them until I mentally nudged them to go on about their business ... *and they did.* Some scurried; some crawled; a few flew. Blackfoot wound figure eights around my legs, but the bat remained. I was no chiropterologist, but I was pretty sure vampire bats were not native to California. I made eye contact with the creature and his breathing slowed. He stopped quivering and settled.

Something ... *shifted.*

It took me a moment to adjust and understand. It took me a moment to realize I could see myself. The vision was distorted infrared; it looked like red-filtered night vision, but it was me, all right. I was seeing myself, Elizabeth Danae Rubis, through the vampire bat's eyes. This small, winged mammal was like a pair of living, breathing virtual reality goggles. I could see through its fucking eyes!

And I looked like hell.

But that wasn't important. It was the first time I had

seen myself since I'd lost my reflection. It had been ... what? Weeks? Months?

I willed the bat to take flight, and it did! I mentally guided it around the crypt. I laughed maniacally. I saw as the bat saw. I saw what the bat saw. I sensed what the bat sensed ... I quickly realized he was a she. "My bad, sweetie," I said out loud. The bat careened out of control, imbalanced by the sound of my voice. I thought, *Sorry!* Like the thing could understand me.

I wondered if all the creatures who'd virtually pledged their fealty to me that night (well, that's what it felt like, anyway) were of the female persuasion. It was a strange thought, but I had a feeling they were. As I contemplated the possibility of this revelation, I lost mental contact with the bat, and my sight was once again my own. She'd found a perch in the rafters as I regained my senses after my trippy experience. What if I could use the bat for reconnaissance? What if I could enter the minds of other creatures and see the same way? There was a charge ... a spark when I stared into the spider's eyes, but no actual connection.

What if I could control them and make them do my bidding?

My mental connection with the bat had given me a headache and fatigued me, an unfortunate side effect. I also hadn't fed yet, so that may have had something to do with it.

The experience with the creatures of the crypt had thrilled and confused me at the same time. I wandered the space and tried to wrap my head around it all. Up to this point, only Blackfoot had shown any affinity toward me, but I just chalked it up to the fact that she was my cat. Maybe she'd missed me while I was playing Halloween with Andrei. That didn't ring true, though. She'd barely tolerated me when I was alive, and now ... well, she seemed to love the new me. A single critter following me around the Bay Area and showing up out of the clear blue sky was one thing; what I'd witnessed tonight was something else entirely.

But then again, so was I.

As I wandered around the crypt, my thoughts wandered as well. I thought about Dietrich and what he had to be dealing with. As I circled and paced, something in my peripheral vision caught my attention, something familiar. *My sketchbook.* Dietrich had left it for me on one of the worn, rotted wooden benches. "That son of a ... "

I flew to it and inspected it. It seemed to be intact. I took it back to my vault, sat cross-legged on the heavy stone lid, and commenced to flipping.

Andrei.

My earliest scribblings were so innocent and typical. Drawings of my house, my parents, and my brothers filled the front pages of the book. Stick figure pets, lemon yellow suns, rainbows, unicorns ...

The drawings became more sophisticated as I got older, and a chill crept into the base of my spine as I saw darkness seep into my chalk and pencil strokes. Each page revealed a deeper shade. I flipped faster and faster until I got to the first rendition, the first sighting, the first evidence of … him.

"Asshole."

Sketch after sketch; different dates, but the same image. A face in a window. His face. Andrei's face.

"Bastard."

The pencil strokes became harsher and insistent, more and more desperate. And then, the last illustration. The night before The Dark Truth.

"Fucker."

I slammed the book and my eyes shut in the same motion. My right eyelid opened a slit as a piece of paper slid from between the last page and the back cover and floated to the floor, landing face down. I heard it slip before I saw it. The chill from the base of my spine rocketed up my back as I flipped it over to find a biographical sketch about Andrei. It was written in Dietrich's hand, and I did a double take at the dates.

> Date: January 3, 1996
> Name: Andrei Marković
> Age: Unk
> Birthplace: Budapest
> Point of Entry: Angel Island
> Point of Origin: Hong Kong
> Year of Emigration: 1910
> Summation: Andrei Marković entered the United States as an immigrant from Budapest, Hungary, in 1910, through

Angel Island. He settled in San Francisco and took an apprenticeship with a local watchmaker. Marković had lived in the Far East for several years prior to emigrating to the U.S. His age was listed as twenty-five, but his real age is impossible to guess. After outliving the watchmaker, Marković blended into the tapestry of San Francisco, moving through the next four decades until?

Strengths: Strength of ten men; appears to have a hypnotic gaze, stealth, and patience; meticulous; rarely makes mistakes.

Weaknesses: Arrogance, never seen during the day (sunlight?), vanity, religious iconography.

Andrei Marković is a serial killer of the most sinister variety, an evil that walks the earth impervious to the ravages of time.

J. Dietrich

I read the paper several times. The dates were very hard to grasp. If Jonas were only twenty-six now, how could he have written this report in 1996? He would have been a child. The authenticity was beyond question. Dietrich had wanted me to find it or else he wouldn't have left it in my sketchbook ... unless it was tucked in the pages by accident.

Nothing about San Francisco Police Department Detective Sergeant Jonas Dietrich made any sense. Not that it had before, but it was getting worse. The mystery deepened and the picture got cloudier. I can't say I'd really ever had a handle on the good detective since he'd crossed my path, but just when it seemed like I was on the verge of understanding, I was denied my *aha!* moment. There was no *"come here, Watson, I need you,"* no Shoemaker-Levy 9. Sure, unraveling Dietrich wouldn't have a global impact on humanity like solving world hunger, but it was important to me. And I was no closer now than the moment I'd read his name online that night at Julie's.

I went back to my sketchbook and leafed through the first few drawings. It seemed like Jonas hadn't gotten why Andrei could pass through the years without aging when he'd written this little biography, but we both knew what he was. I was nine the first time I'd sketched Andrei. Although my artwork was rudimentary when I started my Night Gallery of Andrei Marković, the key features never changed. He'd been the same every time I saw him.

He'd been the same that night before The Dark Truth, the same in the abandoned loft, and the same at the Sutro Baths. The same pretentious prick. Somehow, if I hadn't slaughtered my parents, an "I told you so" still wouldn't quite cut it.

I caught something in my peripheral vision as I sat and reviewed my brain's Andrei file. A crumpled brown paper bag sat on the floor next to my vault. It contained an assortment of clothes and shoes and a smartphone. There was a note.

Elizabeth,

Please forgive my abrupt exit. It's for the best if we don't see each other for a while. I had to make a choice, and you are far more important. I wish I had more time to explain. I wanted to tell you more about Da Rocha and Andrei, but I'm stuck between a rock and a hard place. What I can tell you is, don't trust anyone and keep your head on a swivel. These are dangerous men, but I don't have to tell you that.

You should be safe here for now, but you should try to find other sanctuaries in case you find yourself in trouble. Use the smartphone. You don't need a laptop.

I'm glad to know you, Bet ... just kidding ... Elizabeth. I wish we could have met under different circumstances. I could've really fallen for you.

Always,

Jonas

If I breathed, I would have gasped at that last line. I chuckled at the jab about my name, but my heart sank as I realized the implications. "For a while" might as well have been "ever again." I wasn't sure if I was pining for Dietrich or mourning my human life. Romance and normalcy were things of the past. I had made my peace that I would never be a mother, not that the thought ever really appealed to me. I was attracted to my scruffy detective, and I felt an affinity for him because of everything he had done for me. And not to beat a dead horse, but I felt awful about the position I had put him in. But there was no hope for any kind of relationship beyond what we had experienced already. However, the handwritten note erased any doubt about the authenticity of the page left in my sketchbook.

I was getting thirsty.

CHAPTER IX

I rummaged through the paper sack Dietrich had left for me and pieced together a somewhat presentable black and gray outfit with a pair of flats. There was a box of hair color, but I didn't give it a second glance. I made a mental note to address it sooner than later.

Dietrich's note also confirmed what I knew already, but didn't want to admit. Andrei was still out there. There had been plenty of times when Dietrich's advice about strategically-located hiding places would have come in handy. I quite literally smacked myself in the forehead when I read that line.

I shambled my way to Noriega Street and turned west toward the ocean. I figured I could hitch a ride to the city and search for prey animals.

That was the plan, anyway.

The avenues went up in number as I hitchhiked along

Noriega. I crossed 29th, 30th, 31st, 32nd, and 33rd before a car finally approached. The driver slowed a bit and then gunned the engine. I didn't look *that* bad, did I? A motorcycle roared by, and two more cars ignored me. Finally, just as I crossed 35th Avenue, a beat-up 1974 Ford Maverick crawled to a stop. The driver, a fairly well-dressed man of roughly sixty years old, reached over and rolled down the passenger window.

"Need a lift?"

I hesitated at the sight of the vehicle, and even more so at the hair metal blaring from the stereo. I hadn't seen a Maverick in years, and this was the last place I expected to find one.

"Never mind the car, hop in."

The door creaked and sank with the weight of Detroit steel on worn hinges as I pulled it open. I cringed at the bench seats. It was like a bad 1970s time capsule on wheels. I slid in and slammed the door shut.

"Where to?"

"The City, if it's not too much trouble."

"Yeah, man. Anywhere in particular? I'm headed to North Beach myself."

"Haight-Ashbury."

I don't know why I said it. I didn't know what I would find there. What I did know was that I had spent too much time in the Financial District recently, and I needed to find new hunting ground. My driver lowered the volume because he wanted to chat. I would've preferred the Monsters of

Rock retrospective. He smiled a greasy smile as he drove along, tapping his fist on his left leg to the beat. He spun the wheel with the palm of his hand and turned left, heading south on Sunset toward I-280. Just before we got to Lake Merced Boulevard, I realized he didn't want to chat with me; he was talking to himself.

"Oh, man, oh, man, oh, man, Jimmy, you lucked out ..."

Jimmy continued to keep the beat as he maneuvered the relic of a car along Lake Merced Boulevard. I shuddered at the sight of the water, and I tried my best to ignore him. I hoped he was happy just to be in the presence of a woman; hell, another human being. My intuition told me that Jimmy didn't get out much.

The Maverick rumbled along, and I felt every bump, every rock, every pebble from the heap's bald tires through the worn springs and antiquated shock absorbers right up into my teeth. The road and the rumbling worsened as we wound our way around the lake. Jimmy turned left on Brotherhood Way. This certainly was the scenic route to get to The City and was out of the way if our destination was Haight-Ashbury.

"Um, Jimmy?"

"What's that, sweet cheeks?"

Fuck. Not another one.

"Where are we going? You are driving in the total opposite direction. We could have just hopped up to Lincoln."

His tone changed from playful to menacing.

"Taking a little detour."

Oh, hell no.

I tucked my feet up under my ass and hugged my knees as I looked to my right and saw the Lake Merced Church of Christ and St. Thomas More School. Just past Thomas More Way, Jimmy maneuvered the car off Brotherhood Way and tucked in between Alma Via of San Francisco and St. Thomas More Church. I tried to make myself as small as possible. I was paralyzed in the vinyl bench seat, surrounded by the Father, the Son, and the Holy Rapist. My head swiveled on my neck like an owl on speed as I panicked. I locked in on the cross above the door to the cathedral and didn't immediately notice the drooling, lecherous cretin crawling across the bench seat toward me.

I recoiled against the passenger door as Jimmy approached. His eyes were wild, and a string of saliva oozed from the corner of his misshapen mouth.

"We can do this the easy way or the hard way, honey. God, you're so hot."

"Do what?"

"Oh, I think you know. You need to pay me for the ride. You need to show me a little gratitude. How about a hummer?"

"Fuck you."

"Have it your way."

His hands found my legs. He slid them up my shins past my knees to my thighs as he positioned himself above me. Just as I felt his bony, yellow, nicotine-stained fingers grasp the elastic of my leggings, my instincts kicked in. I remembered who and what I was as I grabbed him by the shirt collar with both hands and pulled down hard, driving his chest into my knees. My superior strength would have to compensate for my lack of leverage. Backing myself into a corner in a Ford Maverick wasn't exactly the smartest thing I had ever done.

I gathered up as much shirt as I could in my right hand and held fast. With my left hand, I reached across my body and fumbled for the door handle. I yanked the chrome lever, and the heavy steel door swung open. We tumbled out of the car in a heap. Jimmy landed on his knees, and I was on my back. He lunged for me. I planted my feet firmly in his chest and kicked. Jimmy hit the Maverick with a metallic *thunk* and crumpled to the ground. I leapt to my feet and towered over this miserable excuse for a rapist.

The church, however, towered over me, and I felt weak. I was still strong enough to keep my assailant in check, but I just couldn't bring myself to dispatch him in the shadow of a house of God. I dropped Jimmy with a good right cross. I spun him around, grabbed him by the collar, and dragged him through two groves of trees to the groundskeeper's work area at the San Francisco Golf Club.

I threw him against a dumpster behind a tool shed. While he sat there stunned, I went into the shed and found a pair of hedge clippers. Jimmy was trying to crawl away when I returned with the clippers.

No longer in view of the church, I felt strong again.

But I was thirsty.

"We can do this the easy way or the hard way, honey. Oh, Elizabeth, you lucked out tonight. God, you're so hot."

"Huh? Wha … ?"

It barely registered that I was mocking my would-be rapist with his own words. He was still stunned that I had turned the tables on him.

"Drop 'em."

"Wha … w-w-what are you talking about?"

"Your *draws*, big boy. You still want me, don't you? You still think I'm *hot*, don't you?"

My lips curled in a sarcastic smirk that revealed my glistening white, razor-sharp fangs. Jimmy scrambled backward but didn't get far. He banged into the dumpster as I sauntered over to him slowly and oh, so seductively.

"It must be killing you that a woman has power over you … "

"You ain't no woman."

I thought about that for a moment. I brought my hand up to my mouth and bit my index finger ever so lightly and playfully. My giggle probably chilled his blood.

"You might be right, *Jimmy*, but I think you can figure out what happens next."

My gaze met his terrified eyes as I crouched in front of him. "Drop 'em."

He scrambled to unbuckle his belt. He pulled his pants down to his thighs.

"And your Underoos."

Jimmy sheepishly pulled his underwear down to reveal his ... well, to call it manhood was being generous.

"Aww ... it must be shy. You wanted to fuck me with that? Oh, please. You couldn't satisfy ... "

It was almost cute.

"Fuck it."

He screamed as I lopped it off with the hedge trimmer.

I could've fed from the spigot I made with the gardening equipment, but that would have been too close to what he wanted me to do in the first place. Tilting his head to the side, I leaned in and opened a vein in his throat.

As water flowed with the *shick-shick* of the sprinklers on the green, the would-be rapist's blood flowed into my hungry mouth. The pulsing of the sweet nectar synced up with the *shick-shick-sshhhhick-shick-shick* until his heart slowed to a pace that could no longer match the sprinklers'. The staccato water burst at the end of the cycle coincided with the end of Jimmy's life.

I stood up, wiped my mouth with my sleeve, and dragged Jimmy to the pit where the golf course stored the fresh strips of sod. The dead piece of shit rolled fairly easily with no blood in it. He landed on a roll of new grass with a soft thud. I turned on a heel and went back to the Maverick.

CHAPTER X

Several thoughts rolled along the synapses of my brain as I slammed the door shut and brought the car to life. A deliciously evil grin curled my lips as I looked up at the cross over the entrance to the St. Thomas More church. I felt powerful, energized.

"Fuck you."

I was mad at myself for getting into that situation in the first place, but what really bothered me was my initial reaction to Jimmy's advances. As much as I had become something else and was still becoming, the last vestiges of my humanity were still hanging on for dear life. I thought I'd shed them when I'd dispatched Billy and his family. But, thankfully, my new instincts had kicked in just in time. I don't think he would have gotten much farther with the human Elizabeth before she would have commenced whupping his ass, but still, I couldn't let these momentary lapses, when I reverted to humanity, become any more of a problem than they already had.

And what the fuck was the deal with the church? I knew I was still a baby, but the power it held over me was like nothing I had felt up to this point. My anxiety was more than just a bit disconcerting; it was downright frightening. It was the closest I had come to consecrated ground. The cemetery ... the abandoned crypt I now called home ... both forsaken by their denominations. They may have sat upon consecrated ground at one time, but no longer. They had been defiled and ransacked, and they held no sway. But an active, vibrant Catholic church? The only other time I had felt something like this was that night I was attacked by the hunter. The cross ... the crucifix he wore ...

Haight-Ashbury was going to have to wait until another night. I was going to spend the rest of this one scoping out and creating a network of sanctuaries. I couldn't afford to get caught too far away from my home base. And since every resting place I had so far had been compromised, setting up several into which I could duck for cover in case of an emergency seemed like wise thinking. Who said I couldn't take advice?

I wasn't behind the wheel of that trashy, piece-of-shit relic of bad 1970's car manufacturing five minutes before longing for the fine German automobiles I had boosted recently. Why did I have to get picked up by Jimmy the Retro Rapist, of all people? That hunk of steel might as well have been held together with bailing wire and chewing gum.

Once I got it above 45 mph, it shook like a rickety old wooden roller coaster. I thought the fenders and bumpers were going to vibrate right off, taking the teeth in my head with them.

Being recognized was a real risk no matter where I went, but San Francisco was a big place. I decided to head for Lori's Diner. I needed some place open twenty-four hours with Wi-Fi. After finding an out-of-the-way parking spot, I tried to keep a low profile. It was a bit more bright and commercial than I would have preferred, but I liked the retro feel, and it was easy to get to. I had frequented the joint when I was … um … alive. More than one client had sucked down a milkshake while listening to one of my advertising pitches.

I needed a place to plot and scheme, somewhere to game plan my house hunting, as it were. Zillow didn't exactly have listings for vampire sanctuaries. And even if they did, it would involve a financial transaction and ownership or a lease agreement. I was in more of the vagrant/squatter category.

After settling in a booth in the back corner, I pulled out the smartphone Dietrich had gifted me. A meticulously appointed server danced over to my table.

"Can I get you something to drink, hon?"

Hon. Normally that would bother me, but in a place like this it seemed more like an affectation than typical *I've-been-doing-this-way-too-long* waitress speak.

"Just water for now, please."

"You got it. One H_2O coming right up."

After finding the Wi-Fi settings and discerning the diner's network, I logged on and started searching. I kept it to a twenty-mile radius and started with abandoned structures. As the waitress delivered my water and took an order I never intended to touch, I scrolled through maps and photo galleries. A few locations in and around North Beach looked promising. I wished I could have stayed at the Grandi, but it was too touristy, too busy. Bayshore Roundhouse was the ideal spot, but Andrei had compromised that one. And the SFPD surely knew that one as well.

My smartphone was inadequate for the level of strategic planning I needed to do. Sure, it had a maps app and GPS, but I needed a 2D navigation system and art supplies. I needed to go old school. The GPS would help me find the locations once I mapped them out, but until then, I needed to channel my inner cartographer.

The waitress gave me plenty of side eye as I left without touching my food. I hadn't even sipped at my water. The look I gave her told her not to worry about the check. The bell above the door jingled my departure as I stepped out into the night. The Maverick was just a shitty as I'd left it, but it would have to do. On the way back to Pacifica, I stopped in a convenience store. The clerk barely glanced up as I picked out some colored markers, push-pins, and a roll of Scotch tape. I breezed by the check stand and snatched a California map from the metal rack on the counter.

"Um, excuse me? Miss? You need to pay ... "

Halfway out the door, I spun on a heel. My hard glare met his wide eyes.

"*Don't.*"

The clerk froze, his mouth agape, and I returned to my hooptie. It took a second to turn over, and I had to pump the gas a little, but the old Ford fired up. I didn't know how long the clerk would stay like that, but I really didn't care. Pretending to be human and paying as I went was getting old, and frankly, I was done with it. The episode with Jimmy had woken me up. The funny thing is, I didn't know if he had been referring to himself in the third person or if Jimmy was the nickname for that miserable excuse for his manhood that I'd unceremoniously removed with the clippers. The bottom line was, as much as I had embraced my new life and what I needed to do to survive, I still hadn't come to grips with my true nature.

From the incident on the rooftop with the vampire hunter to that failure of a sexual predator, my human nature had gotten in the way. Feeding on the living blood of human beings was a way of life now, and I knew I was still evolving. My moment with the critters in the crypt and my strange attraction to Christina were proof positive of that. I felt less and less human, but some of my reactions to certain situations were troubling.

With Da Rocha, I had let my guard down. That had to have been him in the alley. How long had he been stalking me, hunting me? I knew I would cross paths with him again. It was only a matter of time. And I needed to be prepared.

Jimmy had been random, and I certainly hadn't expected him to attack me. That could have been avoided. I needed to take control of my circumstances. Why was I hitchhiking? Why was I depending on anyone? Dietrich's departure, although my fault, had left me alone and cut off from any assistance.

As I drove, my grip on the steering wheel tightened. The tiny hairs on the back of my arms and neck stood on end, as a Cheshire Cat grin curled my lips and exposed my teeth. My fangs, ever so sharp and long, extended. I felt their razor points with my serpentine tongue. My head tilted back; I let loose a maniacal laugh and hit the gas.

After I'd stashed the car and got back to the crypt, I broke out my supplies. I scotch-taped the portion of the map depicting San Francisco to the wall and stepped back. The 2D nav system was definitely the way to go. I could see the entire area and cross-reference intriguing locations with my smartphone. Then, I could GPS the directions to each spot. The reservoir crypt would be the central base of operations, and I would radiate from there. Between sunlight and vampire hunters, I needed to be able to get to sanctuary quickly.

I really needed some string or yarn, but the push-pins and markers would have to do for now. Before long, the denizens of the crypt had gathered 'round to watch this crazy bitch's arts-and-crafts skills. I drew circles and pounded pins into the wall with my fist. Before long I had quite the plan of attack.

"Whaddayathink?"

My question was answered with a few clicks and *squee*s, but nothing that indicated understanding or approval.

"Well, I think this plan just ... might ... work." The last word coincided with one last push-pin jammed into the map in North Beach. It had been a long night, and I was ready for some rest. After sunset, I would head out in the Maverick and scout these locations. If they suited my purposes, I would shore them up and outfit them for my needs. As for my current sanctuary, I puttered around, setting up an early warning system of debris. The only problem was my catatonic state during my rest periods. There was no way I could hear an intruder. Even if I had a helper, I doubt he or she could wake me from that deathly sleep.

Blackfoot appeared from nowhere and jumped into my sarcophagus. She meowed at me and shot me an expectant look.

"Okay, okay. I'm coming."

After climbing in with the feline, I pulled the stone lid semi-closed to give Blackfoot enough room to slither out during the middle of the day if she were so inclined. I absentmindedly scratched her between the ears until I was lost to the black abyss.

CHAPTER XI

I awoke surprisingly refreshed. The cat was gone, of course. My daytime respites were not exactly what I would call restorative or recuperative, except for when I was recovering from gunshot wounds. I touched my hand to my belly where my father had shot me. Not that I blamed him; I would have shot me too, daughter or no daughter. To him, I was a fiend, a thing, the boogeyman. Not the baby girl he'd brought into the world and raised. Of course, he was proud of his sons, but I knew I had been his favorite, even if he'd never said it out loud. Not that I remembered what had happened that night.

The other gunshot wounds I'd suffered at the hands of the police had almost completely faded, but even though it was no longer visible, the one inflicted by my daddy would always be there.

I shook off the emotions like cobwebs and cleared the

path to the cathedral. Then I summoned the vampire bat. As I felt the shift, I shuddered until the connection was complete. I willed the bat to fly around the abandoned church and a one-block radius. The creature screeched and complied. The beat of its wings and its heart thundered in my head, but the vision was crystal clear. I could once again see as the bat saw. As the flying mammal made its circles, I saw nothing of particular concern. After I released the animal, I fell to the floor with a raging headache. Black liquid oozed from my nostrils.

"A nosebleed? A fucking nosebleed? Really?" But that's not really what it was. It couldn't be. My heart didn't beat, blood didn't flow, and this sure as hell didn't look like blood. More like motor oil with way too many miles on it. After wiping my nose on my sleeve, I used the smartphone's camera to take a picture of the map and headed out to scout sanctuary locations. I knew it would bother me, but my first stop was Moss Beach. Only two people knew about that spot—Julie and Dietrich. Julie was dead, and Dietrich was … well, he was in the wind. I figured I could make it work temporarily, and it was not too far from my present digs. I wanted to make sure these hideaways were easy to find and get in and out of. That little wine cellar in that abandoned house on Moss Beach had been perfect. And who would think I would return?

It may have looked like hell, but the Maverick ran well. The throaty engine had great pick up and responded when I put my foot on the accelerator. The house was as I had left it, right down to the break in the chain at the entrance to the drive. I parked the car on the seaside and cringed at the sight of the ocean. The interior was still nasty, and I debated cleaning it up. But then I thought, "What's the use?"

What I did do was rig a way to keep anyone in the house from opening the trap door to the wine cellar from above. After clearing the path to the door for clean ingress and egress, I lingered in the doorway of the room where Jules had put me through the wall. I chuckled to myself at the memory and then practically bounced out of the house to the car. I scribbled on the paper map with a Sharpie and marked the Moss Beach location as complete.

It occurred to me that for the first time since Andrei had turned me into … geez … the word still bothered me … a vampire, I had a plan. After I created this network of hiding places and sanctuaries, I would lay claim to a hunting ground and find a way to sustain myself and stay off the radar of the law and certain vampire slayers. Everything up to this point had been reactionary, not proactive. I needed to get ahead of some things, do some strategic planning, and find a way to survive like Andrei had all these years. He might be a douchebag, but he must have been doing something right to last decade after decade.

I wondered if Andrei had encountered Serge Da Rocha at any point during his misbegotten existence. He must have. Andrei was good, but he wasn't that good. Da Rocha had found me fairly easily, but then again, I wasn't exactly what you would call stealthy. My kills were out in the open, and some were high profile. How the SFPD hadn't swept me up in their dragnet, I'll never know. Dietrich had something to do with that, I'm sure, but his layer of protection was gone, and I had to fend for myself. It was only a matter of time before Dietrich's old buddy Tim, or Da Rocha, or even Andrei would find me and try to end me one way or another.

I ruled out the abandoned boat at Point Reyes, not because it was right on the shore or too touristy, but because it was just too inconvenient. It was nice to know it was there, just in case, though. Drawbridge was next on my list. I was hoping to find it in pretty much the same condition as the Bayshore Roundhouse had been, dilapidated but habitable for someone like me. The rusted hinges of the Maverick's heavy steel door screamed their displeasure as I slammed it shut. A plume of black exhaust billowed out of the tailpipe as the engine roared to life.

"Great. How much longer before you fall apart?" I asked the relic as I gently caressed the worn steering wheel. The forty-five-mile drive to Drawbridge on Station Island was not unpleasant. The wind blew through the open windows and rusted holes in the steel. I reached up to run my fingers through my hair, and then I remembered it was cropped short. Rubbing the side of my head, I wondered if it was growing. The moon hung low in the sky, and I knew I wouldn't be able to accomplish my entire goal in one night. My purpose had distracted me from the need to feed, but as

I looked for somewhere to stash my Ford POS, the familiar twinge crept into the back of my throat.

I figured I had time for one more stop, and I was going to need find a portable blood bank along the way. The water surrounding this one didn't make me happy, but I thought it might discourage some folks who were interested in locating Yours Truly. Too bad there weren't any more duck hunters. I could've done some hunting of my own, but all that was left were ramshackle wooden buildings and ducks, of course. I had my pick of the twenty-four cabins, some in better shape than others. Evidence of squatters, transients, and assorted vagabonds was in almost every structure. Unfortunately, that's all there was. Part of me hoped against hope that I would get lucky and find an itinerant of some variety to feast upon.

The ghost town offered much by way of buildings to explore, boardwalks to dance on, and bridges to skip across. I twirled and sang and hopscotched without a care in the world. This abandoned town was a sea of tranquility smack in the hubbub of the Bay Area. It was a welcome respite from the hectic pace of the last several weeks.

So many municipalities and bergs all connected by freeways and byways. Hustle and bustle at all hours of the day and night from the Carquinez Bridge north to Gilroy south, and from the peninsula and Pacific coast west all the way to Tracy, Modesto, Stockton, and Manteca east all faded away in the distance. Drawbridge and Station Island were shrouded in darkness. Street lamps, headlights, and brake lights were barely visible and twinkled in the distance.

Dancing in the moonlight and spinning with eyes closed, I lost track of where I was and lost my footing. I fell into a creek. For several panicky moments, I couldn't move as I sank like a rock to the bottom of the creek bed. As soon as I had regained control of my limbs, I started thrashing like a toddler who had never been immersed in water before. I forced myself to relax and descended the three feet to the silt once again. The water felt heavy, and I felt heavy as the water filled my lungs. The moon taunted me as it hung in the midsummer night sky. A single air bubble escaped my nostril and floated to the surface. It hovered there for a moment, tempting me, teasing me, until it popped, and I blinked.

So this is how I go. This is how it ends. After all I've been through. The Dark Truth, Andrei, Dietrich, the killings, my parents …

The water weighed me down. I couldn't move. I was paralyzed. There wasn't much of a current, but it was enough. Running water. *Fuck me.* Just the thought of it had been enough to give me pause. The skittish car rides over bridges across the ocean with Julie, and then alone. Hell, the pool at Julie's apartment complex had scared the shit out of me. So much of what I was was myth, folklore, mystery … I had no idea what was true, and I was learning this lesson the hard way. The school of hard knocks had already taught me about religious iconography. I was undead. I walked the earth beyond the grace of God. The encounter with Da Rocha and later at St. Thomas More had drilled that into me.

But what else was true? A wooden stake to the heart? Well, that would pretty much take anyone out. Decapitation? Removing the heart? All pretty much standard for ending someone's life. Garlic? Meh. I had instinctively known to avoid so many of these things without understanding why. It was a reflex more than anything. I thought the water would be an ally here, the isolation even more so. But, yet again, I allowed myself a moment to be human, and look what that got me. How many times was Christopher Lee dispatched like this in those old Hammer *Dracula* films? At least once, if memory served. Seriously, why couldn't becoming a vampire come with a brochure, a handbook ... something?

As much as all these different scenarios kept crawling across the bottom of the screen in my head, the inescapable reality was that I was fucked. If death didn't take me, then madness surely would. First the thirst, then Lord only knows what. I prayed for the permanent blackness to come. I wished for it. I longed for it. Sweet release had to be better than insanity. How long would I last as a ravenous revenant? A shell; only a remnant of what I used to be, roaming the suburbs of Fremont and Milpitas, only to be gunned down in a cul-de-sac as I disemboweled some house frau's Pomeranian. If I could have shuddered, I would have.

As the moon set, another terrifying thought crept into

my overactive imagination. What if this creek was in prime alignment with the rising sun? What if there weren't any structures to block the sun's ultraviolet rays? Poached vampire. Hard-boiled vampire. Vampire al dente. What a fucking way to go.

Well, if you have learned anything about me, you know I wouldn't give up that easily. I thanked my lucky stars I didn't need to breathe. After lying at the bottom of this fetid creek for what seemed like hours, I decided I wasn't going out like that. It was going to take more than heavy water to keep me down or end me. Gathering all the strength I could muster, recalling every crunch, every hanging leg raise, every pelvic tilt I had ever done, I willed myself to sit up. My shoulders lifted a few inches, but that was it. You know how when you can't fall asleep, you try to get each body part to relax? I tried this technique, only in reverse. I balled fists and pushed. My arms rose and shot out toward the surface. They shook from my hands to my shoulders as my abdominal muscles contracted and my torso fought the weight of the liquid. The current pushed me back down toward the creek bed. A garbled, gurgled primal scream coincided with the single greatest expenditure of energy of my entire existence as I powered my way to a standing position.

The dingy water swirled around my legs, and I doubled over and coughed the foul substance out of my lungs.

"FUCK! Goddammit, what the hell was that?"

Nobody but the ducks and the crickets answered me. I sloshed and splashed my way out of the creek. Standing on the bank, I bent over again, put my hands on my knees, and expelled the rest of the water from my system. Judging by the moon and the slightest hint of the sunrise on the horizon, I needed to find shelter and fast. There was no way I could make it back to Moss Beach or the church at the reservoir by daybreak. I found an old zip-up sleeping bag in one of the more complete cabins. Making sure it was empty before I crawled in, I zipped it up completely. Not one centimeter of Elizabeth was visible or exposed.

CHAPTER XII

Sunset came quickly. The days were getting shorter, and the nights were getting longer. This was the natural order of things. The earth would make its relentless elliptical orbit around the sun while spinning on its axis, regardless of what God's creatures, even the forsaken ones, did on the planet's surface. The rising and the setting of the sun, the moon and her cycles, the tides, continental drift, animal migration … all these natural events would continue in perpetuity regardless. The planet would do its best to clean the air and the water with its natural climate cycles, no matter what man put into the atmosphere.

But me, well, I was a different story. I wasn't natural. I was an aberration … an apex predator who didn't earn her place at the top of the food chain through generations of evolution. An apex predator felled by a fucking creek. Some apex predator I was. As much as I had learned already, and as much as I knew from instinct, I would have to gain some valuable knowledge in a hurry. I would have to assume everything about vampires in every book—both fiction and nonfiction—and every movie was true. From silver and garlic to wooden stakes and crosses, and running water to obsessive-compulsive counting, I had to work off the assumption it was all true. Every last bit of it, even the shit that didn't make any damn sense.

I turned all of this over in my head as I snuggled up in the sleeping bag after waking from my preternatural slumber. I didn't want to get up, I didn't want to face whatever was next. I just wanted to curl up in a ball and sleep.

That wasn't an option. The events of the night before had kept me from feeding. I unzipped the sleeping bag and squirmed my way out of the feather-stuffed chrysalis like a demonic butterfly emerging from her cocoon.

I was thirsty.

This was going to be bad.

That smoker's ache crept into the back of my throat. The hair trigger to my temper was pulled back, and I was jittery. I frantically tidied up the cabin before settling in the driver's seat of the Maverick. The engine took a little coaxing and a few extra tromps on the gas pedal before it turned over, and again I wondered how long she'd keep running. Gravel, dirt, and muddy spray spewed from the back tires as I blasted out of Drawbridge and headed toward Pacifica.

It was just after dusk, and Bay Area traffic was exceptionally bad. Brake lights in front of me and headlights from oncoming cars tormented my overly-sensitive eyes. The glacial pace of the evening commute and the increasingly uncomfortable need to feed were driving me toward a road-rage incident of Biblical proportions that I could not afford. I needed to stay under the radar and off the radar guns of any California Highway Patrol speed traps.

Before my impulse-control problem could rear its ugly head, the Maverick betrayed me. A plume of black smoke coughed out of the exhaust, and the car lost power. I stamped on the gas to no avail, and all I could do was guide the jalopy to the shoulder of the freeway. US 101 North was the last place I needed to stall out, but here I was, just north of 237.

I popped the hood and was immediately engulfed in smoke and steam. The motor apparently had blown and overheated in one fell swoop. It continued to knock and ping and shudder for several seconds after it shut off. I kicked the left front tire, like that would help.

In fact, I wasn't exactly sure what to do. I couldn't call AAA or the CHP, or any other alphabet soup for that matter. Californians had a reputation as the worst rubberneckers in the history of ever, and they did not disappoint. It was as if they had never seen a disabled vehicle before. With my back against the smoking hunk of junk and the bottom of my right foot resting against the left front fender, I watched car after car crawl by. Hardly anyone carpooled. Solo driver after solo driver, men and women of all ages and walks of life in every make and model imaginable rolled by like I was a wild animal on their Serengeti safari driving tour.

I folded my arms and watched them as much as they watched me. I'm pretty sure I made a nine-year-old girl wet herself after she stuck her tongue out at me from the back seat of an SUV. I responded by hissing and baring my fangs. Mature, I know.

Between the cloud of smoke and steam and making up road-trip games like "scare the piss out of the brat," I didn't notice the BMW pull up behind the Maverick. A professional-looking woman eased out of the car. She looked to be in her mid-thirties. Four-inch heels, a gray pencil skirt, and black sleeveless top. She shouted at me. "Car trouble?"

The wind created by the cars rushing by blew her dirty-blonde hair into her face. "Need some help?"

I had to resist the urge to make a smartass comment because I wasn't about to look a gift Good Samaritan in the yap, even though I wanted to see how many passersby I could terrify.

"Yeah. I think the engine blew."

"Well, that sucks. Isn't there anyone you can call?"

I shook my head "no" as I stood there with one arm wrapped around my midsection and my right elbow resting on my left wrist, chewing on my right thumb.

"C'mon, hop in. I'll give you a lift."

"You sure it's no trouble?"

"Not at all. We girls have to stick together, don't we?"

I nodded and made my way to the passenger side of the red two-door coupe. My would-be savior slid into the driver's seat and slammed the door shut. Turning to me, she said, "I'm Sarah."

"Well, hello, Sarah. I'm Elizabeth. I really appreciate this."

"Don't mention it."

Sarah pressed the ignition start button, and the BMW's engine sprang to life. The stereo blared some God-awful twangy country tune. Sarah used the steering wheel controls to turn the stereo down to an imperceptible volume … for her, anyway. "Sorry."

A sheepish grin pursed my lips as I stared at the rubber mat beneath my feet. The turn signal made a loud clicking noise as Sarah flicked the plastic stick on the left side of the steering column. She eased the car out onto the roadway as I turned away from her to look out the passenger window. My head snapped around as Sarah started to interrogate me. What was I doing driving such a car? Where did I live? What did I do for a living? Why was I so disheveled? Was I okay? She talked a mile a minute and hardly let me get a word in edgewise.

But she was beautiful. Stunning, in fact. I couldn't see it before with the wind blowing her hair in her face, but I noticed she had exceptionally smooth, sun-kissed skin. I didn't feel like playing twenty questions, but then again, she wasn't giving much time to answer. As annoying as that trait was, Sarah was instantly likeable. And attractive.

My new friend reminded me of Julie in some ways. Sarah wasn't a bubblehead, but she was on her way. She had the type of energy Julie had, an effervescence. And she had this pull like Christina had. Maybe it was the thirst. Yeah, that was it. My eyes took her in, all of her, from the top of her head down to her high-heeled foot on the gas pedal. She was fit; there was hardly an ounce of body fat on her. As I scoped her out, she droned on and on as she effortlessly navigated rush-hour traffic.

As tight-lipped as I was, Sarah was forthcoming with information. I learned quite a bit about her in just a few miles. In fact, she never did ask me where I wanted to go. She was too busy alternating between grilling me and flooding me with her background. Sarah was a real estate agent. A Los Angeles native. A UCLA grad. Thirty-four years old. Divorced. Ex-husband was a serial cheater. No kids, but she'd like to have a couple before she got too old to chase them around. Loved rom-coms and was happy *Will & Grace* was coming back.

Before long, we were pulling into the three-car garage of a palatial home in Atherton. "The real estate market has been good to me. I made a killing after it rebounded in 2008," Sarah said as she shut the engine off and lowered the garage door behind us.

"I'd say so, more like the Bay Area housing market has been good to you." I raised an eyebrow.

"Meh. Six of one, half a dozen of another. You haven't even seen the house yet."

I had done well in my career; made a fair amount of money, but because of my night terrors and psychiatric needs, I never fathomed owning a house, let alone anything like this. This was opulence.

We entered the house by way of the kitchen, and Sarah punched in the code to deactivate the home security system via a keypad near the door. The open floor plan and the space were striking. The home was well apportioned and furnished. It was straight out of *Better Homes and Gardens*.

"You have a beautiful home, but … "

"Thank you. I'll give you the tour in a minute. Shhh. Look, after seeing you on the side of the road like that, I couldn't just drop you off somewhere, all out of sorts. Normally, I would have just zipped by without a thought, but there was something about you."

"I'm usually a little more put together than this."

"Of that, I have little doubt, my dear."

Sarah pulled a bottle of white wine out of the mini-fridge in the kitchen island and rummaged through the drawers until she found a corkscrew. After pulling the cork on the chardonnay, she took a long draw from the bottle before handing it to me.

I politely declined.

"A teetotaler, eh?"

"Not usually, but … maybe in a bit."

"Suit yourself. More for me." Sarah took another substantial pull from the bottle. She slammed it down on the granite countertop and wiped her mouth on her arm. For someone with money and the trappings it could afford, she wasn't exactly refined or sophisticated. She led me on a tour of the expansive house, taking me from room to room and blathering on and on about the features and amenities as if she were showing it to a potential buyer. She stopped short of raving about the wonderful school district.

"I really don't need all of this, but it helps keep up appearances. It's great for hosting parties."

I froze when she threw open the French doors leading to the backyard pool.

"What's the matter, honey?"

"N-n-nothing. I just don't like water is all."

"Can't swim?"

"That's not it … I … "

"Never mind it, then. C'mon, lots more to show you."

There was an office, a family room, three or four (I lost count) bathrooms, and multiple bedrooms. The size and scale of the place was staggering. The events of the last hour or two were a welcome distraction. I hadn't thought about my car situation or the thirst since the Maverick's engine blew. Since it wasn't my car in the first place, it couldn't be traced back to me.

"What are you going to do about your car?"

"Huh? Car … ? Oh, yeah. Um, I guess I'll have to have it towed. I don't think it'll run again. I'll have to junk it. May I use your phone?"

"Yeah, there's an extension in the master bedroom."

Sarah threw open the double doors to the master suite.

I picked up the cordless receiver from the cradle next to the bed and pretended to call AAA. Sarah was none the wiser, as she had gone back to the kitchen to retrieve her bottle of wine.

The bedclothes were as luxurious as any in a five-star hotel, and she was certainly a fan of big, soft pillows. Sarah found me sitting on the edge of her bed. She had two wine glasses in one hand and the bottle of chardonnay in the other.

"You sure you won't join me?"

"Maybe a small glass."

She poured the wine and handed me a glass. After putting the bottle down on a dressing table, she kicked off her heels and paced the room, sipping her wine. I feigned taking a sip of mine.

"You need a shower."

Sarah led me to the master bedroom's en suite bathroom with the soaking tub and spa-inspired shower. She reached for my top, and I recoiled. "I got it, thanks," I snapped rather sharply.

"Okay, okay. I'll be in the bedroom. Holla if you need anything." She giggled and left me to shower in peace, or so I thought.

I got water flowing, shrugged off the irony, and picked a temperature north of one hundred degrees. The cavernous shower featured six water jets in the walls and a digital panel that controlled the water temperature and pressure from the jets. After stripping off every stitch of clothing and neatly folding it on top of the closed toilet lid, I stepped into the streams. I found shampoo and shower gel in built-in cubbies, and started the most amazing shower. I had just finished shampooing my hair and rinsing the soap out when a very naked Sarah slipped in behind me.

Rather than recoil as I had when she tried to undress me, I welcomed her presence. She had cupped some shower gel in the palms of her hands. I arched my back and leaned into her as she soaped me up. I let her expert hands explore and caress my body. After the events of the past couple of days, especially the accidental dunking, I was pretty grimy, and it had been a long time since I had been pampered.

As with Christina, I again found myself attracted to a woman. Was it sexual? Not exactly. Sensual was more accurate. I turned around, and Sarah and I were chest to chest, slick with suds. The attention, the affection, the attraction was genuine. Sarah's hungry mouth found mine, her probing tongue found mine, her hands found my ass.

The thirst was starting to build again. My throat burned. My skin tingled. I shivered.

My hands found the scruff of Sarah's neck, and I broke the kiss with a sharp yank as I pulled her head back. My lips caressed her neck. My fangs found her jugular, and I bit down hard. The sharp canines pierced the skin, I felt them puncture the vein, and Sarah gasped in ecstasy. Her sweet, life-giving blood flowed into my ravenous mouth and down my throat. It spilled down my chin and my chest, smeared across Sarah's breasts, and mixed with the suds and hot water, flowing down our legs to the drain.

"Oh, Beth … "

"Nobody calls me Beth."

Sarah's rapturous moans and heavy breathing quickly turned to wild panic as she realized I wasn't going to stop and my bite wasn't meant to excite —well, not her, anyway. Her moans were replaced by my animalistic, predatory grunts. I had two fistfuls of her hair and her head pulled back as I slaked my thirst at the puncture wounds in her throat. She tried to pull away, but her feet slipped out from under her and she fell. I refused to let go. Sarah tried to scream, but no sound emerged. No one would have heard her anyway. Between the shower jets and where the master bath was situated within the house, we were pretty sound-proofed.

Sarah went limp as I licked what blood I could from her neck and chest. Her breathing became shallow, and her heart slowed. I lapped up the last of the crimson fluid as her heart pumped the final ounces out of the holes in her neck. Her head lolled to the side, and the light in her eyes went out. Grime, soapy water, blood, and Sarah's life swirled down the drain as I shuddered and moaned with ecstasy. My nerves were on fire, my loins were engorged, my nipples were granite hard, and I couldn't help but run my hands over my body with a mixture of blood, water, and soap as I enjoyed my vampiric climax.

I finished my shower leisurely.

After toweling off and griping about not having a reflection, I spent the rest of the evening shopping Sarah's spacious closet. I found a duffel bag and started filling it with blouses and trousers and shoes. As I shifted hangers around and sifted through the outfits, I struck pay dirt. Sarah and I were pretty much the same size with a few exceptions. Some of her shoes were a bit tight or dainty, but there were a couple of pair that fit well enough. Thank God for small miracles. What had Julie said? "Beggar vampire bitches can't be choosers?"

Ever since that night at The Dark Truth, clothing had been an issue. From hospital scrubs at the morgue to the few items Dietrich had managed to scrounge for me, I looked more like a street urchin than a vicious night stalker. Well, that was about to end. I pulled out a pair of black leggings, thigh-high patent leather boots with four-inch stiletto heels, a sleeveless black mini-dress, and a three-quarter length patent-leather trench coat. *Thank you, Sarah!*

After laying the outfit out on the bed, I dressed slowly, rolling the leggings on like a Hollywood starlet in a 1950's romance. The mini-dress slid effortlessly over my head, and I relished the metallic sound as I zipped up the boots. Topping it all off with the trench coat, I was sure I looked positively badass. To be quite honest, this was the first time since waking up in the morgue drawer that I felt whole. But that wasn't exactly true now, was it? I was developing new abilities and starting to find my niche. I wasn't done. I was still *becoming*.

As I brushed my hair the best I could and styled it by feel alone, I came to the realization that attractive, fit, strong women gave me the most intense rush because their blood was the most electrifying. That's why I took Christina when and where I did. That's why I didn't mind the shower with Sarah. That was the best theory I could come up with.

It wasn't a sexual thing. It was a power thing. There was something else, though, something in their blood that I couldn't quite put my finger on. Another thought zipped through my brain, a darker thought, and I shook my head to make it stop. "No, no, couldn't be," I said, as I put on a pair of one-karat diamond stud earrings.

Before I left Sarah's palatial home, I decided to cover my tracks and give myself some time. After finding her laptop, I opened her calendar and checked her appointments. I sent e-mails to her clients and cleared her calendar for the next few days.

A part of me thought about staying at Sarah's for a while, using it as a base of operations and a comfortable safe haven, but I was afraid someone would stop by or, worse yet, had a key. It just wasn't worth the risk.

Besides, there was a hot BMW coupe in the garage waiting for me.

"Fuck."

I realized I had left the smartphone Dietrich had given me back in the cabin on Station Island. After my little swim, I hadn't been thinking straight. The map with my potential hiding places was with the phone.

"How could I be so fucking stupid?"

This was the end of the bullshit. This was the end of forgetting and getting distracted and being careless. No more. Despite my issues, I had always been a true professional. Andrei may have driven me to the therapist's couch, but I'd overcompensated by being a driven career woman. I needed to put that will and determination to good use now.

I had come to grips with what I was and what I needed to do to survive. But I was still making rookie mistakes, and one of those lapses in judgment would get me ended. Back to the program. No more targets of opportunity. Develop an MO. Find a hunting ground and get off the fucking radar. Simple enough.

That was the plan, anyway.

CHAPTER XIII

Sarah's BMW fit me like a glove. From the solid "thunk" of the door to the well-appointed interior, I once again wondered why I had never owned one of these. The leather-wrapped steering wheel was comfortable in my hands, the bucket seat hugged my hips and posterior, and I felt like I didn't have to adjust a thing except the rearview mirror. My right hand grabbed the mirror's frame and tilted it. All I saw was the headrest for the driver's seat, a stark reminder of my state of being.

The lack of a reflection distracted me as I started the car. The garage quickly filled with exhaust. *Dumbass.* I'd forgotten to open the garage door, dammit. I fumbled in the interior of the car until I found the opener. Smoke billowed out into the driveway as the door rolled up. The way that car burst through the cloud, you would've thought I had just broken the sound barrier as I blasted out of the garage in reverse.

I left the exhaust, that beautiful house, and Sarah behind as I headed toward Drawbridge to get my stuff. The car responded to the subtlest of movements and was a dream to drive. It was a far cry from the Maverick, which I caught in my peripheral vision as I zipped by on US-101. It was right where I'd left it. Right where Sarah had picked me up.

This time, I parked closer to the cabin where I'd spent the day. My stuff was nowhere to be found. The last thing I needed was for someone to find the phone with my sanctuary planning in it. I paced, I stomped, I cursed at the sky. I searched other buildings, and I even looked around the spot where I had gone for my swim.

"Fuck."

Realization set in that my smartphone had to be in the Maverick. Mud and gravel spewed behind me as I peeled out. The car fishtailed as the tires found purchase on solid pavement. Risking a speeding ticket, I raced back to the jalopy on the side of the road as fast as I dared. I parked on the shoulder a little bit beyond the Maverick and hopped out. It didn't take me long to find what I was looking for. After pocketing the phone and removing any traces of evidence of my presence, a tractor-trailer whizzed by, forcing me up against the piece-of-shit 1970's relic.

The trucker blared his horn as I flipped him off and shouted a stream of obscenities at him. "Asshole." I pounded my way back to the red coupe and slid into the driver's seat. *Like buttah.* The drive back to the abandoned church in Pacifica was thankfully uneventful. I had half expected John Q. Law to pull up behind me as I was rummaging through that heap on the side of the road. I was frustrated with the drama, and I needed a respite.

As soon as I'd stashed the car and gotten back to the cathedral, I descended into the crypt and took stock of the situation. It was time for another reset. Everything was as I had left it. Nothing was out of place, and had I been able to breathe, I would have expelled a sigh of relief.

Before long I was sitting cross-legged on the stone cap of a vault and flipping through my sketchbook once again. Blackfoot appeared and settled next to me on the slab. I scratched her between the ears with my left hand and turned pages with my right. The sketchbook quickly became a flip book as I animated my drawings of Andrei. I stopped at my most recent, the face in the window. It was my most mature drawing of him; the most complete, even though it had been put to paper in haste. After years of sitting in pitch meetings, I had learned to get my ideas down quickly.

Seeing these drawings made me shudder. Rage welled up inside me as I recalled all those nights when I'd seen him, and nobody had believed me. All those nights I'd known someone had been in my room. All those nights he'd hovered in the air outside my dorm window at Pepperdine. All those hours in therapy. How many sleepless nights? How many hours of my life lost?

My thoughts wandered to Christina and Sarah. The questions turned over in my mind like the pages of sketches. For the life of me, I couldn't wrap my head around why I had been drawn to them. I had an idea. Virility and success had a different effect on me than the forlorn and worthless. From the bros who picked me up at The Dark Truth, Billy, and my younger prey to the Willy Lomanesque failure of a salesman and the Ford POS-driving wannabe rapist, there was a certain pleasure in taking sustenance from some more than others.

But the two women were different. After Sarah, I'd chalked it up to the attractiveness of strong women. Not that being a waitress or a hostess was a bad thing, but Christina wasn't exactly a captain of industry. Sarah was a prominent real estate agent with the house and the car and the clothes. They were both beautiful and sexy. I tried to think of other things they might have had in common.

A chill crept up my spine, inching its way from vertebrae to vertebrae, from the sciatic to the long thoracic nerve …

"No."

A shiver shook my shoulders and head.

"No fucking way."

They were tainted.

That had to be it. They had been bitten. And they had lived to tell the tale. That's why their draw was so powerful. This was a revelation. This was also a disturbing proposition. Who had preyed upon them? Andrei? Dietrich had a history with Christina. Maybe that was why. Andrei had attacked her, and Dietrich had investigated while he was on the fiend's trail. Logical explanation. And Sarah had simply survived. It still didn't make any sense. Neither fit Andrei's type or his MO. They didn't look anything like me. Julie didn't either, but he had made an exception in her case. I was no expert, but Andrei was very much a serial killer, and predators like him rarely hunted outside of their preferences. At least that's what all those true crime TV shows had taught me.

Being attracted to Andrei's survivors made some kind of twisted sense.

Maybe there was another vampire in the area.

I put the sketchbook away and found my way to the roof of the church. I wanted a good signal while I planned for my next excursion. Haight-Ashbury intrigued me. I had a deliciously wicked thought about the denizens of that historic, iconic neighborhood. I called it a night and retired to the crypt after making some mental notes. A sly smile curled my lips as rest came.

CHAPTER XIV

Shortly after arising from my deathly slumber, I made my way to the iconic Haight-Ashbury neighborhood. This place had certainly changed since the Summer of Love in 1967. Adjacent to and right across the street from Golden Gate Park and the Conservatory of Flowers and Bison Paddock—yes, bison as in buffalo—was where the hippies and flower children had given way to homeless runaways and street performers. The house where the Grateful Dead had once lived was now a landmark. I shook my head at the thought.

The vibe at night was more reminiscent of its heyday; at least, that's what I surmised. I was too young to really know. What I did know was that the grit and raw energy of the Flower Power days were long gone, and I really didn't care for what had replaced it. As much as I enjoyed San Francisco and as much as I'd had to mingle in such circles when

I worked in public relations, I'd never cared for the high-end shops and boutiques. The cafes were okay, I supposed. The cost of real estate was another matter altogether. There was a reason Californians were leaving the state in droves. I thought about my tasty realtor as I parked the car in a public garage off Parnassus just south of the Kezar Stadium.

I walked east on Parnassus and took a left on Willard, made a right on Frederick Street, strolled over to Stanyan Street, and made another left. Three blocks north lay Haight Street. I strolled by Amoeba Music, a McDonald's, and the Cha Cha Cha; crossed Shrader Street; and gagged my way past Escape from New York Pizza. Fucking garlic.

The Loved to Death curiosity shop beckoned to me. In life, this place had never appealed to me. Oh, sure, I had watched the *Oddities* television show and was fascinated to learn about this shop, but the macabre and the morbid had never appealed to me. Books and movies were more than enough to satisfy those entertainment needs. But now, well, now was a different story.

Allowing myself the indulgence of window shopping only, I peered in the window for a good long while. Animal taxidermy adorned the walls throughout the shop. If it had antlers, its dead stuffed head hung here. I could make out a gemsbok and a wildebeest, skulls and tentacles, and birds with two heads.

A full-size human skeleton stood sentry in one of the front windows. Funny. This is probably what I should have looked like by now. Instead of dead in the box decomposing, I was wandering the streets of The City subsisting on living human blood. I made a mental note to visit the shop another night.

I was getting thirsty.

The Red Victorian hotel, with its nineteenth-century aesthetic and themed rooms, was intriguing to walk by. I wondered what it was like to stay there, and in my current state of being, I probably would have fit right in. The vintage clothing shop in the front of the hotel and the one on the corner piqued my interest. I was shopping all right, but not for clothes.

The street was claustrophobic from Amoeba to Magnolia Gastropub and Brewery. The buildings were on top of each other. If they didn't share a dividing wall, the alleys were uncomfortably narrow. After spending so much time in confined spaces, the tight confines of the Haight made me uncomfortable. The wider Masonic and Clayton cross streets climbed up steep hills, and Cole led straight to Golden Gate Park, offering some breathing room.

As much as the shops and topography caught my attention, it was the denizens of the neighborhood that really grabbed me. I started a different kind of window shopping. Numerous cars lined the street, and license plates from faraway states like Illinois and New York were interspersed with the usual suspects, California, Oregon, Nevada, and Arizona. All pedestrian varieties strolled by. New parents pushing a stroller with a tiny newborn passenger. Young gay and straight couples in love walking arm in arm or holding hands. A quartet of teenage boys skateboarding. A bicycle pizza delivery guy. You name it; they passed me in either direction as I began the hunt.

Most of the shops were closed, but the bars and pubs teemed with nightlife.

A young female singer and a somewhat older acoustic guitar player on the corner of Haight and Clayton entertained a small crowd of onlookers that had gathered to listen as they performed 1990's female grunge covers. I thought of the musicians who had walked these streets fifty years ago. The talent. The influence. The impact ... and now, we were tortured by the wailings and screeching of an urchin and the out-of-tune strumming of her presumed boyfriend.

As tempting as it was to rid the world of these two hacks, I was concerned that they might be missed. What if they were regulars here? What if locals knew them and expected them to be here? Bringing attention to myself had become enough of a problem. Flying under the radar, going incognito, staying in the shadows ... these things were important. Bumping off this neighborhood's version of the Bushman would probably be a bad idea, not that these two struck me as pillars of the community.

No. I needed to find someone who wouldn't be missed. Someone with no ties, no roots. Someone not from here, someone who didn't belong. Someone the police and the media wouldn't think twice about. I shivered at the thought of feeding on the homeless. Dirty, disgusting, urine-stained nastiness. No. I needed something younger, more vibrant, more full of life.

I wandered the streets of Haight-Ashbury for hours. Across Central to Broderick and back again along Page and Oak, I walked and pondered all the while, keeping my head on a swivel, my ears pricked up, and my eyes wide open. Not only was I on the hunt for prey, but I would not be taken by surprise again, not after Serge Da Rocha had almost ended me.

And then I found her.

In an alley between Page and Oak, a young girl of about twenty or so sat on the ground between a dumpster and a stack of wooden pallets. She wore torn and tattered blue jeans. I wasn't sure if her life had caused the wear and tear or if the jeans were just made that way. She wore a black Misfits t-shirt that had holes for more than just her neck, arms, and torso. Her toes protruded over the end of flip-flops that were two sizes too small. Her feet were filthy. Her once white sandals weren't anymore. Her thick, curly, dirty blonde hair hadn't seen shampoo or a brush in weeks.

My boots pounded the pavement until I stood over her, lorded over her. After a long moment, she looked up, her puffy eyes bloodshot from crying. Her cheeks were soiled except for two lines where streams of tears had eroded clean streaks. She was pretty in a sad, dingy sort of way. I pitied her.

"What's your name, child?"

What the hell was I thinking? Child? Really? I went with it.

"Whitney."

"Do you have a last name, Whitney?"

"Harkendorff."

"That's a mouthful. Where are you from?"

"Um ... Noe Valley."

"No, no, honey. You may live in Noe Valley, but where are you *from?*"

"Wyoming."

"Wyoming? What the fuck are you doing here?"

"I'm an artist."

That seemed to be the draw to Haight-Ashbury these days. Writers, artists, they all thought they were the next Jack Kerouac or Margaret Keane. Lord knows they couldn't afford to live in North Beach. Many of them ended up on the streets, some as young as twelve. Runaways, transients, drug addicts, wannabe novelists and painters and sculptors, idealistic and full of life when they got off the bus, became crushed dreams and disappointment in the flesh living on the streets within months.

Girls like Whitney were a dime a dozen, but there was something different about her, something in her eyes.

"Why are you crying?"

"Th ... th ... they took my stuff. My phone, my paints, my brushes, my chalk ... my sketchbook."

Well, hell.

"Wait here."

CHAPTER XV

It didn't take long to find Whitney's attackers. They were in an alley a few blocks away. Street kids, like Whitney; four boys of different ages. The youngest couldn't have been older than twelve. Shabby rags that were once shirts and pants and jackets draped over their malnourished frames like oversized dresses on hangers. Their cheeks were sallow, their eyes sunken into their skulls. They almost looked undead ... like me.

I stood at the mouth of the alley and took up an aggressive fighting stance. The ragamuffins were fighting over Whitney's bag.

"Hey, that's mine! I'm the one who snatched it!" the youngest called out.

"So? You want it, come and get," the largest, oldest boy taunted, holding the backpack high in the air by one of its shoulder straps.

The two other boys, much closer in age, looked like brothers. Judging from their mannerisms, fraternal twins wasn't a bad guess. They were sniggering while they watched their companions tussle over the pack.

This could have been an episode of *The Little Rascals*, for fuck's sake. Why I'd developed such an affinity for Whitney so quickly, I'll never know. I'd never developed quick attachments or become fast friends before, so why now? Whether or not I spent one more second with her was irrelevant. These thieving punks needed to be taught a lesson. We artists needed to look out for each other.

"Hey! Give me that bag!"

"What's it to ya?" the boy with the backpack responded.

"It doesn't belong to you."

"Oh, yeah? Says who? You?"

"You know damn well who it belongs to, and I am going to give it back to her."

"Come and g—"

Before he could finish the sentence, my preternatural speed propelled me to the boy in a flash. We were nose to nose before he realized I had even moved.

"Get her, Kelly!" one of the twins called out.

Kelly launched a haymaker at me with his free hand. I caught his wrist effortlessly, twisted it behind his back in one smooth motion, and drove his face and chest into the pavement.

"You're hurting me!"

"No shit, Alfalfa."

"Huh?"

"Oh, never mind."

Tossing the backpack aside, I feasted on Kelly and the twins. It was like the Livermore boutique all over again. I was out of control. This time, it wasn't thirst that drove me; it was rage. My attack was savage, wanton. Blood, flesh, and homeless urchin parts were everywhere. The asphalt and the walls of the two buildings on either side of the alley were sprayed with crimson.

The youngest of the four boys was frozen with fear as his pals lay broken and dead at his feet. He stood with his mouth agape, no words escaping. He was paralyzed. I stooped down in front of him and met his eyes.

"Now, are you going to steal again, little boy?"

He shook his head rapidly.

"Are you going to bother girls anymore, you little shit?"

Again, with the rapid head shaking.

"Good. Now get the hell out of here."

He was still frozen to the spot.

"Boo."

The boy turned tail and ran out of the alley as fast as his little legs would carry him.

Whitney was where I'd left her, sitting on the ground with her back up against a cinder block wall. A crumpled newspaper swirled on the pavement on one side, while discarded fast food cartons had taken up residence on the other. She looked up slowly when she realized I was standing before her. Her crying had abated and her tears had dried, but she still looked defeated. I thrust out the hand that held the backpack strap. My hand and wrist were covered with the blood of thieves.

Whitney reached out and took her pack from me. She saw the blood on me and searched my eyes for answers. Tears began to flow again.

"How?"

"Never you mind. The important thing is you got your stuff back."

"I don't know how to thank you."

"Oh, I'm sure we can think of something. You hungry?"

"You have no idea."

"Try me."

Before long, we found an all-night diner and settled into a booth in the back. The joint was harshly lit and almost empty. A heavyset trucker-looking guy in a red flannel shirt and the requisite ball cap sat at the counter, slurping coffee and sopping up egg yolk with a gnawed piece of burnt toast.

"Wait here."

I walked to the counter and got the waitress's attention. She leaned over …

"Help you?"

Her name tag said she was Brandi. Her face said she was in her early thirties. I made eye contact and tried to sear my gaze into her brain. Frankly, I was tired of traipsing around like an ordinary human being. The incident with the late owner of the Ford Maverick had changed my way of thinking, once and for all.

"Look here, Brandi. See that girl over there?" I tossed my head in Whitney's general direction. "She can have whatever she wants. And we're not paying for anything. Got it?"

"Y-y-yes, ma'am."

"And when we're done, when we leave, you will remember nothing of this conversation or the two of us. Say you understand."

"I-I-I ... u-u-understand."

"Good. Take her a pot of coffee and leave it on the table, and take her order."

Brandi nodded and walked around the counter into the dining area while I made my way to the restroom to wash up. Whitney may have noticed the blood on my hand and wrist, Brandi was too spellbound to realize it, but I knew it was there. When I returned to the table, Whitney had a table full of food in front of her. A stack of pancakes, bacon, sausage, English muffins, a pot of coffee and a half-empty mug, and a glass of orange juice.

I slid into the booth and got comfortable. Resting my chin on my interlaced fingers and propping up on my elbows, I regarded Whitney with as friendly a look as I could muster.

"What? She said to order whatever I wanted."

"I know, sweetie. I guess you're pretty hungry. When was the last time you had something to eat?"

Whitney just shrugged her shoulders as she shoved another bite of maple syrup and butter-covered flapjacks into her face. She ate hungrily but daintily. This young artist was no slob, just down on her luck. A pang of jealousy came over me while I watched her consume her food. They say variety is the spice of life, but since only one thing served as sustenance for me now, the variety came from the types of people I fed on. Some were more virile and vibrant than others.

"How long have you been in California?"

"About six months."

"Do your parents know where you are?"

Another shrug, another mouthful of pancake.

"Come on, Whitney, tell me your story."

"What do you care? You're just another old person who's going to shit on me."

"Whoa. What the fuck? Listen here, young lady, I didn't have to help you. I didn't have to get you your bag back, and I sure as hell didn't have to feed you. So, you better check yourself. You have no idea who or what you're dealing with, so a little respect is in order."

"I'm sorry. I'm just not used to people being nice to me."

"Look, bottom line is this … you remind me of me. I'm a bit of an artist myself; been drawing for years. I really like to sketch. Everyone has their way of dealing with shit. I draw."

"Me, too!" Whitney's attitude changed in an instant. Her ears pricked up and her face brightened as she realized we could be kindred spirits after all.

"Show me."

My young companion fished her sketchbook out of the

backpack *I* had rescued for her, opened it, and slid it over to me. I flipped through the drawings. Her art wasn't dissimilar from mine, and I could tell she'd had the book for a while; perhaps it was her one and only ... like the one I had been using all these years. Her technique and skill matured page by page, like mine. Pastels and chalk and pencil and ink told Whitney's story, from pastoral Wyoming, a train ride to the West Coast, the Central Valley, and finally, San Francisco.

Despite some nightmarish images of what looked like a boogeyman and scary dark places, the most recent sketches in particular caught my attention. I took my time thumbing through those pages as familiar cityscapes brought a smile to my face. Whitney's style was ultra-realistic, almost photographic. She captured the Bay Bridge and the Golden Gate in great detail. Almost all her drawings were night scenes.

"You don't move about during the day?"

"Too much attention from the authorities during the day. Better to lay low and come out at night. Nobody notices you at night." Bacon, sausage ... slug of coffee. I was really taking a shine to this girl.

"Seriously, why did you leave Wyoming?"

"I wanted to go to art school."

"I get that. Who's the creepy guy in the pictures?"

That took her by surprise. I had my own creepy guy in my pictures. He'd turned out to be real, so I figured her boogeyman was real too.

"Stepfather."

"That bad, huh?"

"You have no idea."

"Fair enough. You don't have to tell me. What about your mom?"

"Fuck her."

"Okay, then."

My problem-solving brain didn't have much of a problem figuring this out. Abusive stepfather, apathetic mother, repressed artist. It made perfect sense. She wasn't the first, and she sure as hell wasn't going to be the last. It reminded me that I had been lucky to have the parents I'd had … until … yeah, well, that wasn't important right now.

"I couldn't get into Academy of Art University, and I ran out of money. I did the caricature thing for a while, you know."

"I know exactly what you mean."

"After a few months, I took up with some street kids."

"I see."

The next several pages of the sketchbook were filled with portraits of skate punks, runaways, street performers and musicians, local business proprietors. Then I froze. A lone drawing on a page chilled whatever now ran through my veins. It was a building, row houses, maybe, and a man … floating in midair … dressed in a trench coat.

I spun the book around and tapped the page violently with my index finger.

"What the fuck is this?"

"What … ?"

"You seem to draw what you see. What the hell is this?"

"Oh, yeah, that. So, I came around this corner, and there he was, floating. He was looking in the window. I couldn't see in to see what he was looking at. It was like he was this supernatural peeping Tom. I had been hanging out with a bunch of kids who were smoking weed that night, so I thought maybe I had a contact high or something. I don't do drugs, but I hang with plenty of people who do. It is what it is. I remembered it later and sketched it out. I took a picture, but it didn't come out right."

I flipped the sketchbook back around and studied the drawing closely. The figure floating one story up was all too familiar. The unkempt hair. The raincoat. The pants and shoes. Whitney had captured him perfectly.

Dietrich.

How in the hell was he floating a full story off the ground, and why the fuck was he peeking into a second-story window?

"When did you see this?"

"A few days ago."

It was the most recent drawing Whitney had made.

Jonas, no doubt, was disgraced. There was no way he was still employed by the SFPD, but if he was, he was more than likely suspended pending an investigation into the events at Local Edition. Whatever his predicament, it was my fault. I had compromised him. I'd put him in an untenable situation. He acted to protect me at his own expense. But this … this was something altogether different. The fucker was *flying*.

I really wanted to believe that Whitney had been stoned when this vision presented itself to her; I really did. She didn't strike me as a liar or a drug user. Her assertion that she didn't do drugs was said with sincerity, but she was a runaway. Homeless. She could have been lying for all I knew. Hell, she could have been a professional liar, relying on the kindness of strangers to get by. I remembered a story on the news some years back about a homeless guy in Ohio, I think it was, who made sixty grand a year panhandling. Maybe there was more to Whitney than met the eye. How cynical and jaded I had become.

"Do you remember where this was?"

"Yeah, North Beach."

"Will you show me?"

"Mmmmhmmmm."

Whitney finished her pancakes and assorted breakfast meats, and then ordered a slice of apple pie. Brandi brought it dutifully and smiled at me as she delivered the pie to the dingy runaway across the table.

After inhaling the pie, Whitney took a deep breath and exhaled as she leaned back. She desperately needed a bath and some fresh clothes. And I needed answers.

"Finish up, sweetie, we need to go."

Glancing over at the counter, I noticed Brandi was starting to emerge from the state I had put her in. The last thing I needed was for her to try to get us to pay. I had no money and no plastic. Whitney and I had to skedaddle before the spell wore off. She polished off the last of the coffee in her mug, gathered up her sketchbook and backpack, and we headed out into the night.

Stockton Street.

We walked from the Haight-Ashbury neighborhood to North Beach along Stockton Street. The Financial District end of it and the Stockton Street tunnel had such significance for me now that I had a hard time every time we crossed an intersection and I had to read the street sign. As we approached Union and Washington Square, I started to panic. Anxiety started to flare up as Saints Peter and Paul Church loomed ahead.

I grabbed Whitney by the hand and tugged her to the right.

"Let's cut over to Grant."

"But it's just up ahead, just past the church."

"That's great, but we're taking Grant. We'll double back."

We eventually made our way to Powell and Chestnut. I couldn't bear the thought of walking anywhere near that goddamn church. As we approached, the vista in Whitney's drawing came into view.

"Well, fuck me."

"You wouldn't like it. I'd just lie there."

"Ha ha. Funny. You're not my type. So, this is where you saw Mary Poppins in a trench coat?"

"Who is Mary Poppins?"

"For fuck's sa—"

"Yeah, yeah, this is where I saw the guy ... floating ...

the peeping Tom."

When I'd first seen the sketch, my gut had told me it was Andrei, but my mind had filled in the blank. That's not what was on the page. The levitated figure bore all the hallmarks of one Detective Sergeant Jonas Dietrich. I really wanted it to be Andrei; I really did. That would have made much more sense. With all the other crazy shit he could do, why not fly? Why not float around like a demonic Peter Pan? It would explain a lot, like how he could have peeked into my dorm room window when I was in college.

But Dietrich? As much as I wanted it to be Andrei, and as fantastic as the possibility of a levitating peeping Tom was, Whitney had to have been on drugs when she'd had this vision. There was no other explanation. But considering what I was, how could I really rule anything out? My abilities, my powers, and my very nature were evolving almost on a daily basis.

"Are you sure?" I squinted and crinkled my nose at Whitney.

"I saw him as plain as the nose on your face."

"Whitney, dear girl, I could tell you some things that would curl your toes and put hair on you in places you didn't know you had places. But a floating man in a trench coat?"

"Look ... wait ... I didn't catch your name."

"I didn't throw it."

"W-w-whatever. Look, the dude was floating. I told you. I don't do drugs. I've never done drugs in my entire life. I've never smoked weed, snorted a line, or shot up. Swear to God."

I cringed at the mention.

"And you say he looked just like that? Scruffy, raincoat … "

"Exactly like my sketch."

Her voice trailed off with the last word. Whitney looked down at the sidewalk. She was not used to being taken seriously, apparently, and she didn't take too kindly to my skepticism. Rather than get angry or indignant, she started to shrink back into her shell.

"Now, now, Whitney, honey, I believe you, I just find it incredible, is all. My life is … um … complicated. And I have seen some shit in the past few months. It's just that this is beyond … "

But was it, really? I was communing with bats, for crying out loud. Was Dietrich floating two stories up, peeking into windows, all that crazy of a notion? I subsisted on living human blood. I had murdered people, and, unfortunately, would do it again. So, why were my cop friend's aerial antics so out of the realm of possibilities? A few short months ago, I didn't think vampires existed, and we see how that turned out.

"I know what I saw."

I put my hand under her chin and lifted until her eyes met mine.

"Elizabeth. Call me anything else, and I'll kill you in your sleep."

"Y-y-yes, ma'am."

I might have said it with some measure of jocularity, but I could see in Whitney's eyes that she knew I meant it.

"Was that the only time?"

She nodded. Her eyes welled up with tears and searched mine for what … understanding? Acceptance? Love? I wrapped my arms around her and held her tight. We were very similar, Whitney and me. Alone in the world, orphans of a sort, artists, vagabonds, kindred spirits. The thought warmed me, if I was capable of such a thing, and scared me at the same time. Everyone close to me suffered. Everyone except my brothers, I suppose. Lucky for them, they were able to return to their homes. I couldn't help but feel for Whitney. I was drawn to her, I felt for her, and I wanted to help her. And she might be able to help me in return.

My thoughts drifted to Billy … poor, hapless Billy. Had he trusted me and believed in me, he'd be getting ready to start med school. Instead, he was in a box, six feet under. He'd paid the ultimate price for betraying me. Billy and Whitney were polar opposites. He was a child of privilege and means, and was a poseur and a hanger-on. Whitney was tragic, abused, neglected, and a victim of circumstance who'd tried to get out and make a life for herself. But like so many who come to the big city looking for their break, she'd had her soul ripped out by countless rejections and run over by a Muni bus.

I'd always known my future was in commercial art, advertising, or public relations. I'd made that determination early on. People like Whitney, with their wide eyes and bushy tails and buckets full of idealism and optimism, think they'll realize fame and fortune in this lifetime. That word had new meaning for me. Lifetime.

Now she was a street kid, a modern-day urchin, trying to get by and wondering where her next meal was coming from or where she would lay her weary head each night. We were alike in many ways. I had become a transient of sorts. As each sanctuary was comprised, I had to move on to the next. I never really knew where the next meal was coming from, although I had the skills and means to hunt, and I no longer felt the need to earn a living.

Adjusting to this life was constant struggle. As many times as I had made mental notes that I was going to own my existence and all of the dirty, disgusting things that came with it, I'd have another episode like I'd had with Jimmy. As much as I thought that what had happened with that creep would be the end of my mousy behavior, the proof would be in the pudding.

"Where are you staying?"

"A youth hostel in the Haight. It's not too shabby. It's better than a shelter, and safer."

"I bet. Where can I find you?"

"Buena Vista Park. I like to sit and sketch there."

We walked back to Haight-Ashbury, carefully avoiding any houses of worship, and I dropped Whitney at her hostel. After I told her I would look for her the next night, we parted company.

CHAPTER XVI

I stepped onto the sidewalk from the stoop. I looked to my right. I looked to my left. Then I scanned back to my right. On the corner. A hulking figure. *Da Rocha.*

He flipped his heavy duster backward off his hips like a gunslinger. He pulled two long fighting knives from scabbards hanging off his wide leather belt. Backpedaling, I frantically looked for an escape route. There was no way I could win a fight with a trained vampire slayer. I was unprepared. I had no weapons.

He charged like a bull. Heavy-booted footfalls echoed off the buildings and created a deafening cacophony of sound that hurt ... no, pierced my eardrums. Da Rocha was surprisingly fleet of foot for a man his size. I turned and ran. Breaking into a full sprint in just a few strides, I thought to outrun him. Staring at the ground in front of me, I ran a few blocks before looking up. There he was on the next corner.

"How the hell ... ?"

I banked left down the closest alley, clambered up a fire escape, and found myself on the flat roof of a six-story building. I jogged over to the edge of the roof. A low parapet was all that kept me from tumbling over. This was eerily like my first encounter with Da Rocha. Me, on a rooftop, my back to a wall, under an open sky, with nowhere to go.

Da Rocha's head appeared over the top of the parapet as he ascended the fire escape. I frantically searched for another route, because this one had worked out so well. A utility door looked like a possible exit, but there was no guarantee it would be unlocked. As I scanned my environment, Da Rocha hoisted himself over the wall and rose to his full height. Arms akimbo, knives splayed out at his sides ...

"Elizabeth Danae Rubis."

How the fuck ...

"You are an abomination. You exist beyond the grace of God ... "

"Yeah, yeah, tell me something I don't know, big boy."

"You die tonight."

"I'm already dead."

"I am going to destroy you, once and for all."

"I suppose you're going to do it with those big knives of yours."

Da Rocha wasn't much for witty repartee. The next-door building looked like it was too far away to jump. A childhood memory popped into my head. My brothers telling me, "jump, that's a jump," while we played at a construction site for a new home. I didn't make it and smashed my knee on a cinder block. This was a bit more dangerous and a bit more life-threatening.

An opening presented itself, and I had to go for it. If I stayed on this roof, Da Rocha would make short work of me. Fighting street kids and waylaying the unsuspecting was one thing; taking on this knife-wielding professional wrestling reject was another.

Taking a sprinter's stance, I eyed the building across the way. Screwing my right foot into the roof tar, I steeled myself. My right leg propelled me forward, my left foot hit the surface of the roof, and I pushed as hard as I could. Within four steps I was at top speed. Within ten paces, I was a mere few feet from the parapet. I consciously lifted my left foot, planted it on the stone of the parapet, and leaped.

Halfway across the expanse of space between buildings, something *shifted*.

My body contracted. A membrane of thin skin covered and connected my impossibly elongated fingers. My torso and legs shortened. My hearing sensitivity increased dramatically. I flapped my *wings*.

I was flying.

My eyes did not lie. I saw as I saw when I communed

with the bat at the abandoned church. The visual acuity was unmistakable.

I had transformed into a bat. *A fucking bat.* I didn't know how; I didn't know why. I was mystified as I flapped my wings and flew away from my would-be assassin. I didn't think about it, I just did it; it just happened. Maybe it was survival instinct. The fight or flight response, quite literally. Within a few minutes, the flying felt quite natural, like I was born to do it.

Circling the area, I looked back to see Da Rocha, stone-faced, searching the sky for his quarry. He leaned forward, resting his palms on the parapet as he watched me flap away into the night. And flap I did, all the way back to my sanctuary. This was the second time Da Rocha had caught me unaware. There would not be a third.

After landing on the roof of the church, I looked down at the rooftop, flapped my wings down hard, and willed myself up. My body elongated. My fingers shrank back. My legs grew, and my fur and wing membranes became human skin, hair, and clothes again. That last bit threw me. How was I not naked? How had I not shed my clothing back in the Haight? What the fuck was I turning into?

Coming to grips with vampirism and all its trappings was one thing, but this was a horse of a different color. I was so confused. Reconciling fact and fiction and movies and books with reality was maddening. What was true? What was real? What was folklore? What was superstition? What was I?

I threw my arms back, tilted my head back, and roared. ROARED.

Thunder cracked, a fork of lightning split the sky, and it started to rain. It was pouring within minutes, and I retreated to the dry crypt. There were plenty of leaks and holes in the roof, so my resting place wasn't as dry as I would've liked. The rain subsided as my mood improved. The downpour slowed to a trickle as I took stock of my roommates.

Water dripped from cracks in the ceiling as I surveyed the room. More vampire bats had made the trip from Mexico. More free-tailed bats and a couple of hoary bats had taken up residence in the corners and nooks and crannies where the walls met the ceiling. The insect and rodent population had increased as well, and the arachnids, well … the spiders were quite at home with me. The variety of species was too many for me to count, although it was tempting to try. Forty-three distinct species of spider.

There. Dammit.

Six Mexican free-tailed bats, four big free-tailed bats, and three hoary bats. Dammit. Twelve beetles. Seven cockroaches. Two praying mantises. Five pill bugs. Dammit. Drip. Drip. Drip. Drip. Drip. Drip. Drip. Drip. Drip.

I counted one hundred and eighty-two drips before I lost it. By the time I had finished, stone sarcophagus lids and vaults were in pieces, all but mine. There was that, at least. How much of the night did I lose counting? I'd lost track of what I'd counted and how much, and I had an epic hissy fit. Now the darkness was receding, and that foul orange ball of fire was starting to rear its ugly glow over the horizon. The last few raindrops fell as I took to my coffin.

CHAPTER XVII

When I rose to greet the night, I was shocked by the destruction I had made during my obsessive-compulsive, counting spell-induced temper tantrum. The episode had taken me completely by surprise. I had been able to control this aspect of my condition. I had been able to shake it off when I felt it trying to creep in. This compulsion was strong, but not nearly as strong as the thirst.

My creepy crawly roommates slowly used their preferred methods of locomotion to return to the crypt from the cracks and crevices and the shadows. Fear. Respect. Both. It didn't matter. I was queen of this roost, and we all knew it. They regarded me with reverence as I floated out of the vault and settled softly on the stone floor. *Floa-ted.*

Floated.

Still stunned from the events of the night before, I

couldn't put two and two together, let alone draw any conclusions. What did I know? What did I think I knew? My head ached as I tried to process everything that had happened the night before. Kicking rubble as I paced, the facts still seemed incredible. Starting from the beginning, I verbalized the events in chronological order. It started with meeting Whitney, dispatching her tormentors, and seeing the sketch of Dietrich as a floating peeping Tom, and ended with a confrontation with a vampire slayer and my turning into a bat.

Floating. I had just floated.

There was no way. Whitney had to have been stoned when she'd drawn that sketch. That was the only logical explanation. I was humoring her when she tried to tell me she didn't do drugs. But a kid from Idaho or Wyoming, or wherever she said she was from, living on the streets in San Francisco? There was no way she didn't do drugs.

Jonas's note popped into my head. I felt a tug on my heartstrings as I recalled, "I could've fallen for you." I was tempted to read it again, but my head was filled with too many other incredible thoughts.

I put the sketch and all its implications away in the dark recesses of my mind. The reality I needed to face was that I had turned into a bat.

While making my escape in a transformed state, I had abandoned that sweet car that I had boosted from the tasty real estate agent. However, a thought struck me like a bolt of lightning. Could I transform on demand? Could I just fly to where I wanted to go? Did I become a bat because I was trying to get away, or was it truly a fight-or-flight response? Well, I was sure as hell about to find out.

And where was that damned cat? I hadn't seen Blackfoot in a while. Not that I was worried about her; she could take care of herself, but I had gotten used to having her around, and I missed the little shit.

I made my way to the roof of the cathedral. Whitney was on my mind. Did Da Rocha see us together? Was he now trailing her, hoping to draw me out? He was getting on my last nerve. We were going to have it out, one way or the other. I just preferred it to be on my terms, whatever those would be.

It was not lost on me that I had made it rain. I was the bringer of storms. Funny, now I could see why Andrei was such a pretentious, narcissistic bastard. Falling down the egoist rabbit hole was easy when you could affect the goddamn weather. I was under no illusion or delusion that I could control it. Let's save that for another day. Right now, my concerns were a bit more provincial.

Transportation had been a problem from the very beginning of my, um, condition. Since the night I'd escaped from the morgue, getting around the Bay Area had been a chore. Boosting cars and bumming rides, and sometimes leaving dead people in the back seat, was nothing short of inconvenient. If I could fly ... now, that would be the shit.

What was not going to happen was some half-assed, rookie Spider-Man, bouncing-off-brick-walls, landing-on-cars, web-shooter-practice bullshit. Either this was happening, or it wasn't. I thought long and hard about the events of the previous night. The bat thing had happened without my even thinking. I didn't will it to happen, I didn't do anything special, like stand there tensing every muscle in my body like a five-year-old trying to make a pony appear out of thin air. I mean, who would do that anyway? Seriously.

Running and leaping off a rooftop is what had made it happen. Stretching out for that distant landing spot, that's what had made it happen. Not thinking about it, that's what had made it happen. So here I was on another rooftop, about to throw caution and my body to the wind.

"Fuck it."

Within five steps, I was at top speed. I planted that left foot again and pushed, my arms stretched out …

… flying was **GLORIOUS**! The wind through my fur, buffeting my wing membranes. You really have no idea until you free yourself from your earthly bounds. Airplanes don't cut it, not even little private planes. Helicopters don't, either. I've been aboard both types of heavier-than-air vehicles, and there is nothing as liberating as unfurling your own wings.

Did I really just … ?

As wondrous and uncannily natural as it was to flap away into the moonlight, it was work after a bit. I had to concentrate on what I was doing, you know, almost like driving a car. Distracted flying is just as dangerous as texting and driving. My hearing as a bat was ultrasensitive, and I almost gave myself whiplash every time I heard a noise that struck my fancy. The echolocation was something else entirely. Sensing the distance between objects in this way was fascinating and frightening at the same time, but it was incredibly useful, and I was thankful for it. I damn near slammed into a wall.

I pointed my twitching nose toward Haight-Ashbury.

Whitney was my priority. I needed to know she was all right. I needed to know that Da Rocha hadn't discovered her and concocted a plan to get to me. I needed … I needed to feed. The further I flew, the thirstier I became.

My new friend wasn't hard to find. She was on a corner, sitting and sketching a pair of street performers. The music and singing were shrill to my bat ears. I landed on the roof of a three-story flat-roofed building. Repeating what I had done on the roof of the abandoned church I called home, I forced my transformation back into human form. Again, I was amazed and mystified that my clothing had shifted with me. But I was a vampire, not a werewolf. *An American Werewolf in London*'s David woke up nude the day after a night of carnage. It was just a film, but early vampire movies depicted shape-shifters turning into bats, wolves, rats, mist, and what-have-you.

There wasn't time for shape-shifting practice. I was worried Whitney would pick up and move off to another spot. The alley between the building I stood upon and the next was empty, and I dropped to the ground as gracefully and as quietly as possible. Stepping out onto the sidewalk from the shadows, I strolled to the impromptu outdoor concert venue up the street.

My patent leather boots came to a shoulder-width stop in front of Whitney. Her photographic drawing ability was stunning. She'd captured the male acoustic guitarist and female singer and frozen them in time. She looked up and squinted as a streetlight above and behind me blinded her and silhouetted me.

"Elizabeth?"

"The one and only. I missed you."

"It's only been a day."

"True. But I enjoyed your company last night. And I've thought about you all day." That last bit was a lie, of course.

"Why are you interested in me? I'm nobody."

"Don't you dare. Don't you dare trivialize yourself. Everything still in your bag? Anything missing?"

"No, it's all here."

"Good. How's the show?" I tossed my head in the direction of the performance.

"Not bad, actually. A little Natalie Merchant, a little Alanis Morissette. She's really on key tonight."

"Scoot." Whitney nudged over and made room for me as I sat cross-legged next to her on the grungy sidewalk. My gaze alternated between her sketchpad and our friendly neighborhood troubadours. My new friend was correct in her assessment. The singing and guitar playing were pleasant, the songs recognizable and enjoyable, and for a moment, we were transported back in time to the summer of love and Haight-Ashbury in its heyday. I closed my eyes, and Whitney and I swayed back and forth to the music.

"Anybody bother you last night? Today?"

"Like who? Those kids who took my stuff? I haven't seen them around. You must have put the fear of God into them."

"More like the devil," I mumbled.

"Excuse me?"

"Nothing. No, not those kids … Anyone … else?"

"No, no one."

"Has anyone been … following you?"

"No, no, not at all. Say, what's this all about?"

"Oh, nothing, sweetie, nothing at all. Draw … listen to the music … don't mind me."

We listened, we sang along, we enjoyed.

After a time, Whitney finished her rendering and closed the sketchbook. The vision of Dietrich hovering in the air popped into my head. I resisted the urge to grill Whitney about it again.

Did I mention I was getting thirsty?

"Hungry?"

"Famished. I haven't eaten since … "

"Don't finish that sentence, I don't wanna know."

Same all-night diner, same brain-scrambled Brandi. Whitney ate heartily, but less than she had the night before. I put my elbows on the table, interlaced my fingers, and rested my chin on top of my hands as I regarded my young friend with affection.

With a mouthful of French toast, Whitney garbled, "Why did you ask if I was being followed?"

"Don't worry about that now. It's not important."

The girl slurped her coffee, belched, and said, "I could be a lookout or something … "

Bacon, sausage, more French toast slathered in butter and maple syrup …

"Don't worry about it." My stern tone convinced her to drop the subject. After Whitney had finished her meal, I walked her back to the hostel.

"Will you visit again?" She was staring at the ground, acting like a child asking for a piece of candy.

"Would you like me to?"

"Please?" She looked up. Her eyes met mine, and tears welled up in her lower eyelids.

"Of course."

Whitney turned on a heel and bounced into the entrance to the hostel as I turned my attention to other matters.

The street minstrels Whitney and I had enjoyed earlier were just packing up as I wound my way back to my original landing spot. I hid around the right angle of a nearby building and watched them stow their gear. If I were a smoker, I would have lit up a smoke, but cigarettes had never appealed to me. Okay, well, there was that time in college, but that's not important right now.

Their Mini was parked in the alley around the corner from where I spied. They didn't talk much, and if I were to hazard a guess, I'd have said they were in the middle of a spat.

"Let's just get out of here, Danielle."

"Fine," Danielle responded in an indignant tone.

They were so wrapped up in getting the guitar in its case and scooping up the cash they had earned that Danielle and her accompanist didn't notice they were being followed. I crept as quietly as I could, but the crinkle of my patent leather boots and jacket threatened to give me away with each step. I froze each time I thought I was a twitch too loud.

As I started to run toward them, I broke into a full sprint, my feet barely touching the pavement. By the time I got to the Mini, I was ... *ravenous*.

The guitar player—I never did ascertain his name—stood at the back of the vehicle as Danielle opened the hatch. Just as her male companion slid the guitar into the storage compartment, I pounced and tackled them both, driving them into the trunk space. It was the larger Mini, and the rear seat was folded down.

Leaping into the vehicle, I growled ... or was it a purr? Saliva dripped from my tongue.

"Hi!"

They both screamed when they saw what had knocked them into the car.

The hatch swung shut behind me when I leaped into the trunk. I pinned them to the bed of the trunk with my preternatural strength. Try as they might, they could not escape my grasp. Any passerby would have thought some wild sex was going on in the diminutive vehicle with all the shock absorber and spring-wrecking bouncing going on.

Blood sprayed and splattered on the windows and upholstery as I opened veins and arteries and temporarily slaked my insatiable thirst. The growling and screaming and thrashing subsided as the blood flow slowed to a trickle out of their bodies. I licked my chops and savored the essence of the musicians. I hadn't tasted creative types before. Oooh. They were different. Their energy spiked mine. Perhaps it was their talent; perhaps it was the blood of young people.

Whatever it was, I liked it.

I tilted my head back and savored the sweet nectar as it poured down my throat. I usually enjoyed the moment I broke the skin and made the blood flow more than anything else. But this time … this time, it was after the frenzy, long after the dying started. Sometimes, it was about the stalking and toying with my prey, and enjoying that moment, but when I was this thirsty … well, get a squeegee. The hair on my arms, my sex, and the back of my neck stood on end and tingled as orgasmic moans escaped my throat. A full body shudder started at my toes and finished at the top of my head. I really didn't know what to make of the different climaxes I experienced with each of my … victims.

When I finished with the street performers and lapped up the blood from their throats and the leather seats, I clawed at the latch. Narrowly avoiding sitting in a pool of blood, I crawled over them, pausing to rifle through the guitar player's pockets to find his keys, and made my way into the driver's seat. The engine roared to life as I turned the ignition over. This wasn't the first time I had driven around San Francisco with dead bodies in the back seat of a car, but I sure hoped it would be the last.

There was a spot in North Beach I had been wanting to investigate as a possible sanctuary, and the night was still young. I backed the Mini out of the alley and pointed it toward the Barbary Coast Trail.

CHAPTER XVIII

There was an art supply store on Pacific Avenue that had a secret underground with possibilities. I parked a few blocks away on Balance Street. Making my way to the roof was easy. All the buildings along Pacific were adjacent to one another. A nearby parking garage gave the purchase I needed. From the top level, I was just a few rooftops away from my destination.

A service entrance door lock was no match for me, and I forced my way in. Thankfully, they hadn't thought to alarm it. A door at the bottom of the utility stairwell met a similar fate, and I made my way into the main sales area. The local art and the endless rows and racks of supplies gave me pause. The pens, pencils, paints and brushes, canvas, sketch pads, and spiral-bound books of blank pages made me ache for my creative outlet. But my objective lay deeper.

I found my way to the lower level. More supplies—hard-core art supplies—sat undisturbed on shelves upon shelves. I fingered numerous items and thought about an epic shoplifting spree. But my objective lay even deeper.

In the corner, almost hidden from view, was a stairwell and a rickety old wooden staircase. I was getting quite used to those, but I don't think I'd ever say I was fond of them. Winding my way down to a lower level, I recalled the walking tour of North Beach that Julie and I once took. That's how I'd known this place existed and learned about the lower level. Mainly a tourist attraction and a photo op for tour-goers, the basement spoke of an earlier time, when wooden sailing ships ruled the harbor and the Sydney Ducks terrorized the neighborhood where I now sought refuge. But my objective lay deeper still.

When I'd taken the tour some ten years earlier, I'd lagged behind the group, lingering longer than I should have. But I had discovered something. A trapdoor. Sure, there was one in the ceiling that led up to the street, but I had found one in the floor. A door long forgotten; at least that's what I'd thought.

Feeling around with my foot, I'd thought I'd found the edge. How no one knew about this was beyond me, but I'd dropped to all fours and found the four sides and dug out the rectangle. I'd swept away the years of dirt and uncovered a pull ring. I'd grabbed it and yanked. It had taken a few hard tugs, but it eventually had given way and lifted. Years of dust and dirt and … yuck had come up with it. A cloud of … well, a cloud, had emanated from below. Another dark, rickety wooden staircase into a dank abyss.

The wood was rotted and the footing was treacherous, but I soon found my way to the bottom. The hollowed-out space, the void, was more than large enough for me to use if I had to. This was a relief. I now had three strategic locations I could use to hide from the sun or certain jackass vampire hunters I didn't care to mention, if need be. Now that I was done playing *Lara Croft: Tomb Raider*, it was time to stash a Mini and a couple of dead bodies.

There was another nearby parking garage that would serve my needs. After climbing my way out of the bowels of the art supply store and satisfactorily hiding the trapdoor, I made my way back to the Mini and drove it to the garage at Jackson and Kearny. After finding a nice corner spot on the second level from the top and covering up the bodies the best I could, I made my way to the roof.

I pounded to the east end of the roof of the parking garage and assumed the sprinter's starting position. In five steps, I was flapping into the night back to my sanctuary. The distance was longer than I had covered previously, yet I wasn't fatigued.

Looking at The City this way was quite different through bat's eyes than human ... rather, vampire eyes. The echolocation helped me navigate and kept me from crashing into buildings. My vision had become much sharper since the *turning*, with colors more vivid and details more pronounced. But as a bat, it was almost like I was in *The*

Matrix. Edges of objects jumped out of a monochromatic world that appeared charged and electric, and the echolocation enhanced that visual information and gave me feedback pulses to fill in the blanks. It didn't help me avoid flying through a large cloud of gnats, though. Bleah.

Bat, vampire, whatever. I was still a girly girl, to a point.

What else could I become? Shape-shifting was another new concept, and I still hadn't mastered the others yet. Oh, sure, I had survival locked down, but other elements of this existence still eluded me. Hell, my impulse-control problem was going to be the death of me if I didn't learn discretion and moderation. At least I'd had the good sense to stash my victims tonight. They would be missed. Not for long, though, as I was certain other traveling minstrels would take their place, eking out an existence singing for their supper on a street corner in the Haight-Ashbury neighborhood. The two I'd dispatched weren't runaways or local homeless people. Somebody would come looking for them. The denizens of the area would notice they weren't around anymore. I had thought that when I first saw them and ruled them out. But then when I saw them again, I just didn't care. The thirst had me. I just hoped the neighborhood wouldn't care, and if it did, not for too long.

When I returned to my resting place and my *human* form, my thoughts turned to Whitney. I sat on the edge of my vault and wondered about my intentions toward the young girl. As tempting as she was, I had no desire to feed on her. Okay, that was a lie, but I did not intend to feed on her. My affinity for her trumped any murderous attraction I may have harbored.

But what was I doing, really? Did I want her to be another Billy? A lookout? A daytime guardian? Could I turn her? Could I live with myself if I did? She could have easily become Billy's successor. Whitney didn't have any real ties to anyone. Nobody was going to come looking for her, which made it less likely she'd betray me the way Billy had. Although I didn't feel remorse for the way I'd handled things with Billy, it angered me that he'd betrayed me and hadn't trusted me. I'd never forget the look on his face that night when he was sitting in the back of the squad car and I tussled with that SFPD SWAT team. Asshole. Fuck him.

Whitney's hopes and dreams at her age resonated with me more and more as I spent time with her. But I really didn't know how long I could go on with her this way. I did enjoy her company though.

I spent the rest of the time until sunup sketching a portrait of my new friend in my old sketchbook, as the creatures of the crypt turned the endeavor into a spectator sport.

CHAPTER XIX

So many things have been inspired by dreams. Great works of art, writings, political aspirations, career choices. I still don't dream. As a vampire, my resting hours were spent in a zero-consciousness state with my subconscious registering no activity, and one of the few things I could liken it to was being blackout drunk. It was like all those times you'd glance at your phone while you were driving, just like you weren't supposed to, and read an email or a tweet or something, and before you knew it, five miles and who knows how many exits had flown by.

My thoughts, my synapses, my daydreams, my memory processing ... it all took place during my waking hours. Making memories wasn't an issue. I was making and retaining plenty of them. There was no new memory loss with my condition. I had no idea how to make a vampire; thus, I had no idea how Andrei had made me. But I remembered that night at The Dark Truth, then waking up naked and bound in that abandoned loft ... Andrei's smug little fucking face ... the EMT's attempts with the defibrillator. I remembered it all ... except ...

It was like my body and mind shut off during the day. It was like I was ... dead.

Obviously, this wasn't the first time I'd turned these thoughts and questions over in my head, but spending time with Whitney had brought me back to them. I wondered what she dreamt about. I wondered if her dreams inspired her art or if all she saw now were nightmares.

I was happy the days were getting shorter, which meant I could venture out a little earlier each evening. Although I was not conscious during the day, my body was perfectly synchronized to the rising and setting of the sun. The vulnerability factor was not lost on me and was why I was so torn about Whitney. Did I dare tell her about myself ... who and what I truly was? Should I try to recruit her to become some sort of apprentice to the devil? Or did I just continue to play mentor and guardian for a while longer?

Blackfoot leapt into my lap as I contemplated these things. "Where the hell have you been, you little bitch?" I scratched her behind the ears and stroked her from the top of her head to her tail. My attentions were met with purring and that mystical cat ass raise. "Where do you go, little miss?"

Considering the contemplative state I'd found myself in, Blackfoot's timely reappearance was comforting. In all actuality, I really didn't have much of a choice than to just be a friend to Whitney and help her along for a bit. While I was doing that, maybe I could figure out a long-term solution for her.

I took to the skies, hoping Whitney would be easy to find once again. Little did I know I was about to have issues of my own.

Travel time as the bat flies ... well, I wasn't really sure. Transforming into a flying mouse and back again fully clothed was a mystery to me; one of many mysteries, but somehow I didn't think the molecular rearrangement that took place each time would extend to a smartphone or other accoutrements. I really hadn't noticed how long it took. I just knew I was flying faster than freeway traffic, and it was only about fifteen miles or so to my destination.

Following Route 1 was the easiest thing to do since it took me right to Golden Gate Park. All I had to do from there was head east toward Haight-Ashbury. The moonlight reflecting off Lake Merced to the west was beautiful. I flew into the park, banked right, and instantly regretted it. A hawk swooped down out of some cloud cover and struck me square in the back with its talons. Its powerful wings pushed us toward the ground. I flapped my wings in an effort to get away, but the bird's grip was impossible to break.

The raptor landed with me beneath it. It panted with its long thin tongue hanging out of its beak as it tried to catch its breath after the tussle. Forcing myself to relax, I stopped flapping and struggling. The bird looked down at its prey, regarding me, searching for the perfect spot to tear at me with its sharp beak and devour its meal.

Once again, I forced the transformation. I pushed until I could feel my legs elongating, the wing membranes and protracted fingers retracting. The fucking three-pound bird was startled now that I had turned the tables. Rising to my full height, I held the hawk upside down by its legs. The damn thing was just a-flapping away and craning its neck, trying to take a chunk out of me.

I thought I was slick and tossed the thing in the air like I was some sort of half-assed juggler. I thought I could just grab it in midair, but I thought wrong. It went right for my face. I turned my head just in time. I reached out and grabbed it by the wings just as its talons tore at my coat. Holding it by the chest with my left hand, I reached up and snapped its fucking neck.

Disgusted with the whole affair, I tossed the bird of prey into a nearby row of bushes. First Andrei, then Da Rocha, now a fucking hawk. Gimme a break. I smoothed myself as best I could and set out to find Whitney. I was sure I was an absolute mess. Gawkers and lookie-loos stared as I tried to turn away toward the buildings and storefronts to hide the worst of my bloodstains and torn garments. I walked faster and faster and did my best to avoid eye contact.

As easily as I had come upon her the night before, Whitney was a bit more elusive on this night. Wandering the streets of The Haight, young people of every persuasion were kicking off their evening festivities. Sports fans who didn't have a ticket to the game streamed into the bars, or maybe the Giants were out of town. It was late summer, not quite time for football. Hell, it could have been a soccer or tennis match they were all crowding around the flat screens to see, for all I knew.

A man with dreadlocks was getting his ukulele out of its case and setting up for an evening of strumming and singing and panhandling. Eight grungy, dirty kids clambered out of a hybrid du jour. I was surprised I didn't get a contact high from the cloud of marijuana smoke that emanated from this nouveau hippie clown car.

They talked of the "old days," when great musicians and drug-enabled or addled free thinkers gathered at Haight-Ashbury and wrote and sang and communed and dreamt of changing the world. I wasn't sure what this current group was capable of, but I was pretty sure a few of them would meet a grisly fate, and quite possibly at the hands of yours truly. The last thought brought a wry smile to my lips.

Musicians were going strong in Golden Gate Park. The sound of bongos and didgeridoos and acoustic guitars became louder as I approached one of the park entrances. The amalgamation of instruments and the cacophony were coming from Hippie Hill, just beyond a small pond and an arched stone tunnel that may have once been a bridge. Although the sun had set, it wasn't completely dark yet, and I found my quarry sitting on the ground in a void between large boulders at the edge of the pond. She was sketching.

Whitney was dressed slightly differently than the last time I'd seen her. She was wearing low-top Chuck Taylor sneakers that might have been optic white once; military-style fatigue pants tied off just below the knee, giving the illusion of capris; and a white tank top. A gray hoodie was tied around her waist.

"Would you like some company?"

Whitney's face lit up when she realized it was me. "Of course! Please sit."

"Thank you. And how are we this fine, unseasonably warm evening?"

"*We* are fine. And it is hot, isn't it? I didn't think summers in San Francisco were this warm."

"It'll be fall before you know it, and then it'll get plenty cold."

"Not like Wyoming. Winters there are brutal."

"I can imagine. What are you going to do in the winter? You can't stay at the hostel forever. As you said, shelters are worse. Have you thought about going home?"

"Home is no good. I'm never going back. You can't make me."

"Hey, now. Remember, I'm the one trying to help you."

"Yeah, I know. I'm sorry. I just don't like thinking about …"

Her voice trailed off, as did her gaze. She looked across the pond and the tunnel as if they weren't even there. Whitney was a million miles away.

In a soft, distant voice, she asked, "Did you hear about Kelly and the Kazmarek twins?"

"Um, who? I don't ... "

"The boys who took my stuff the night I met you. They were found dead in a dumpster a few blocks from where you found me."

"Oh, I don't watch the news. You knew them?"

"Yeah ... no ... I mean, I knew them from around the way. You never did tell me how you got my stuff back."

"You don't think I had anything—"

"No, no, nothing like that. It's just strange, is all."

Changing the subject became a priority.

"Hungry?"

"I thought you'd never ask."

We stood up and Whitney gave me the once over.

"What happened to you?"

"What?"

"Your coat is all torn."

"Oh. Fucking bird."

I shed the coat and tossed it in a nearby trashcan, making a mental note to replace it. I loved that trench coat. Good thing I had something on underneath, not that a topless woman would be that out of place in this neighborhood.

Another all-night diner, another mesmerized waitress. Another plate stacked high with food. A glass of orange juice. A mug of coffee. Whitney ate in near silence as I perused some news websites on her smartphone.

"Three young boys were found dead in a dumpster in an alley in San Francisco's Haight-Ashbury neighborhood. Their bodies were mutilated. Authorities believe that it may be the work of the same serial killer or killers that have been terrorizing the Bay Area the past several weeks ... "

"Disgraced San Francisco police detective Jonas Dietrich has yet to be found. He is sought for questioning regarding an incident at a local theme bar and is considered a person of interest. Dietrich was in the company of a middle-aged woman when the woman allegedly attacked and killed an employee of the establishment ... "

"Fuck me. Middle-aged, my ass." I didn't realize I'd said that out loud.

"What's the matter?"

"Oh ... n-n-nothing. Eat your pancakes, sweetie."

Now I was a million miles away.

Whitney didn't notice that I slid the phone across the table as she crammed forkfuls of syrup and butter-soaked flapjacks into her hungry mouth, slurped hot black coffee, and chugged pulp-saturated orange juice while barely pausing to breathe, while I stared out the window thinking about Dietrich.

The news articles I found were rather disturbing. My indiscretion had sunk Dietrich. He was on the run. A wanted man, a fugitive. A person of interest. He might as well have been a suspect. And he was putting himself on the line for me by not turning himself in. Maybe he was avoiding that for other reasons, like his hunt for Andrei. I knew that singular focus all too well.

My mood shift barely registered with my ravenous companion. I lost track of time while she consumed three plates of pancakes, as well as several sausage links and strips of bacon, and sucked down who knows how many cups of coffee and glasses of orange juice.

Living day to day, from meal to meal like this, had to be hard for the kid. She should have been in college, developing her talent, learning, making friends, falling in love, and dreaming of how she was going to change the world.

Through a mouthful of buttermilk goodness, she said, "I can't thank you enough."

Her voice snapped me back into the now. "Huh? For what, kiddo?"

"Feeding me. Looking out for me the last couple of nights."

A sheepish grin curled my lips. "Think nothing of it."

It was just past ten o'clock when we left the diner and headed back to Golden Gate Park. We walked past the pond and through the stone arch tunnel, along the paths until they gave way to Robin Williams Meadow. Whitney and I reclined on the cool, wet grass and stared at the stars for a good long while. Wispy clouds temporarily obscured the faraway pinpoints of light and the ever-closer moon. I interlaced my fingers behind my head and leaned back, crossing my legs at the ankle, and gazed at the night sky.

Whitney did the same. She took out a cigarette from a half-crushed soft pack and lit it.

"Smoke?"

"No, thanks, sweetie. You know those things'll kill ya."

"Yeah, well, you only live once."

That's what you think.

I was getting thirsty.

We relaxed in the grass until the park closed at midnight and then strolled out to Stanyan Street.

"Another night at the hostel?"

"Yeah, I'm paid up through the end of the month, so … "

End of the month? Shit, I didn't even know what day of the week it was, let alone what week it was. I thought it was July. You'd think I would have noticed while I browsing the news earlier.

"Shall I visit again tomorrow?"

"Yes, please!"

Whitney was a bit embarrassed by the quick enthusiasm with which she'd replied. She looked at the ground, her feet, away, at anything but me. Lifting her chin until her eyes met mine, I said, "It's okay, honey; I'm pretty fond of you, too."

An awkward smile was followed by blushing as Whitney and I parted company for the night.

"Be careful, young lady," I called after her.

"Don't worry, I'll be fine."

Did I mention I was getting thirsty?

I walked west along Lincoln Way past Kezar Drive and crossed 4th Avenue. I re-entered the park at 9th Avenue. I wound my way back to the stone arch tunnel. A man of roughly my age carrying a large bongo strapped across his back was walking in front of me. I broke off the path and climbed up toward the top of the tunnel. Moving without sound and with alacrity, I maneuvered ahead of him and waited.

Just as he made his way past a broken chain link fence at the mouth of the tunnel, I leapt onto his back. The fucking giant-ass bongo was an immediate hindrance, and I regretted my choice of victim immediately. It would not have surprised me in the least if it had said *Giant Ass Bongo Co.* on the side. I hauled him to his feet by the strap of the monstrous instrument and threw him against the wall of the tunnel, shattering the drum. Wood and mule skin and fastenings flew into the rancid air that was thick with the smell of urine and God knows what else. My prey was stunned and too shocked to make a sound. The only noises coming from him were ribs cracking. He fell back to earth, and I moved to straddle him. A pair of young girls headed for the tunnel decided to take a detour as they thought they were interrupting an amorous tryst.

The bongo player coughed, spurting blood that dribbled down his cheek and chin.

"Oh, no, honey. Not yet. Save some for me." I licked my wicked grin with a serpentine tongue. Horror widened his eyes. My fangs and gaping maw were the last things he would ever see.

I ground my sex against his erection … yes, he was hard … and squeezed with my thighs. No true sexual release came, but the electricity that came with ingesting the bongo player's blood, slurping it, really, was better than any traditional orgasm I had ever had.

My physiology continued to mystify me. Why were my kills akin to sexual experiences? I wasn't about to complain. This was far better than ham-fisted romance and penetration attempts by some man who wasn't worthy of me any damn way.

CHAPTER XX

The next several nights were rather enjoyable. I flew to Haight-Ashbury, spent time with Whitney, hunted in the park, and flapped my way back to my sanctuary. Each night we'd put in at a different all-night eatery, Whitney would consume her fill … and later, so would I. We were leaving quite the trail of mesmerized waitstaff in our wake.

Whitney was a pleasure to be around. I had truly found a kindred spirit. The best part? She didn't ask too many questions about Yours Truly. We talked about my public relations career, and I lied, of course. Most of our conversations involved what she wanted to do with her life, her hopes, her dreams. She didn't talk about home much, and I could only surmise that the nightmares she might encounter here in San Francisco were better than the ones she knew in Wyoming.

I developed quite the hunting routine in vast Golden Gate Park. It was much bigger than I'd thought, and the prey was as varied as the citizenry. I tried to focus on runaways, mainly older kids in their twenties. There were some whose folks in Illinois should probably stop worrying about them—the quartet of kids who'd packed up Mom's station wagon with their heads full of dreams and pot smoke. I didn't even bother trying to ditch their car. I'd left it with the doors open and the engine running, if I remembered right.

Whitney didn't seem to care that she never saw me during the day or that I never wanted to visit during daylight hours. She was an admitted night owl, and that was just fine by me. The kid just wanted a confidant. Someone to hang out with for a couple of hours. Someone who didn't judge her. Someone who didn't want anything from her. I figured when she was ready, she'd tell me stories of family secrets and lecherous uncles, an abusive father, and an enabler of a mother. Maybe I'd get the nerve to tell her of my own nightmares ... explain that *I* was a nightmare. Maybe she'd understand. Maybe she'd run away screaming. That I couldn't handle.

After several nights of enjoying Whitney's company, preying on the aimless, and flying back and forth to my sanctuary, I had almost forgotten about Jonas and Da Rocha. That's not true. Jonas was never far from my thoughts. Da Rocha ... well, I actively worked hard to put that asshole out of my mind. There had been no new sightings of the church's top vampire killer since the last encounter. For that, I was grateful.

My cryptmates were a comfort to me, even as their numbers grew. More and more bats, bugs, and rodents took up residence, and I wondered if I were going to run out of space or raise the suspicions of the local Orkin man.

The nights were growing cooler and longer, and I relished the thought of the onset of fall. After arising from my coffin, sketching for a while, and spending some quality time with Blackfoot, I took to the roof and transformed. No birds of prey had molested me since the incident with the hawk. Perhaps word had spread throughout the local food chain about the new apex predator. Or maybe it was because I avoided flying through the park.

Whitney proved to be elusive on this night. Normally I was able to find her rather easily in a few passes over The Haight. Not tonight. I found a secluded rooftop and set down. After transforming, I jumped three stories from the roof to the ground and landed softly. I pounded the pavement looking for my charge. I looked in doorways, alleys, restaurant and shop windows, along the edge of the park, and up the walking path to Kezar Stadium. I searched the usual haunts. The pond, the diners, the hostel … anywhere Whitney and I might have visited.

I wandered for hours.

As I walked along Page Street, I heard a disturbance. It was something out of the ordinary; something different, yet familiar. Trash cans were scattered. A cat screeched. I stopped at a void between two buildings.

A man was on top of a woman. Her left leg was straight out, and her foot was twitching.

A foot covered with a dingy, formerly optic white Chuck Taylor sneaker.

A leg covered with camouflage print capri pants.

The man wore ... well, all I could see was a trench coat.

A well-worn raincoat.

An all-too-familiar coat.

No.

The couple wasn't coupling. This was something else. They were clothed, and no sounds of human passion emanated from them. But I heard soft sucking sounds.

I approached quietly and as more of them came into view ...

"JONAS?"

I cocked my head like a dog as San Francisco Police Department Detective Sergeant Jonas Dietrich raised his head and turned to look at me. His eyes were a shade of red that didn't come in the Crayola box of sixty-four. Blood poured out of his mouth and dripped from a pair of impossibly long canine fangs. He didn't recognize me; the thirst had him. He just stared at me as he stood up. Dietrich was lost in the throes of the wanton bloodlust that cursed us both. He was in a frenzy like I had experienced once or twice myself. That frenzy you don't remember when you also don't remember who you killed.

My attention turned to the woman on the ground.

Whitney.

She twitched ... she convulsed ...

... until she twitched and convulsed no more.

Her white tank top was white no more.

Whitney was no more.

I screamed an impossible scream. Thunder cracked. Lightning tore the sky apart. Heavy dark clouds formed overhead and dumped their payload of water in a deluge.

"What the fuck did you do, Jonas?"

Dietrich was dumbstruck.

"JONAS! You goddamn son of bitch! What the ACTUAL FUCK did you just do?"

The green flag dropped, and my thoughts and emotions raced down the front straightaway. How in the hell was Detective Sergeant Jonas Dietrich a vampire? How long had he been a vampire? Was this a new development, or had he been one all along? Is this why he had been running interference for me?

And poor Whitney. Why Whitney? Was it because she had been palling around with me, or was she a random target of opportunity?

Just as the light of recognition lit up Jonas's face, I forced a transformation and flew off into the downpour. I heard, "Elizabeth ... wait ... "

Settling on the roof of the hostel where Whitney had been staying, I forced myself back to what qualified as human form for me these days. The rain finally subsided as

I calmed down. Oh, did I need to have a think. What the hell had just happened? What the fuck had I just seen?

As was the case more often than not, I had more questions than answers. I had very few answers, actually, but a few hypotheses started to form in my stunned brain. Cooler air was moving in over the warm summer waters of the Pacific. As my head cleared, fog rolled in, and fast. I took some comfort in the blanket of gray that I had undoubtedly conjured with my emotional outburst.

Jonas had to have been a vampire for some time. Why else would he exclusively work nights? Why else would he work the strange and unusual cases? Because he had to and because only he could. But what was his connection to Andrei? Was there one? He'd acted like he didn't know him when we'd tussled at Sutro Baths, yet he had been pursuing the fiend all along. And what the hell was the deal with Christina? Was she an ex-girlfriend or something else? Something … more?

A deep emotional pain settled in. Whitney and I had shared a bond. I had looked out for her while we hung out. I'd made sure she ate. I'd listened to her as she'd shared her deep, but not quite deepest, and dark, but not quite darkest, secrets, and her hopes and dreams and aspirations. We had spent hours together. And time was the most precious commodity. Not gold, not diamonds, not cash, not pork bellies, not oil … time. Considering what I usually spent my nights doing, that I chose to spend time with someone who didn't slake my thirst meant something.

And Jonas had taken her from me.

This was the fourth person close to me that I had lost to this curse. My parents, Julie, and now Whitney. It was easy when it was Andrei to blame. It was easy when I could project all my anger and hatred for my condition onto that smug bastard. But now, hell ... now it was someone I cared about, someone who I thought cared for me, creating all kinds of hate and discontent due to *his* condition. Dietrich hurt me in ways I didn't think were possible. He'd lied to me. He'd betrayed me. He'd killed someone I ... loved.

"Hello, *Elizabeth.*"

CHAPTER XXI

He came out of the fog like he was made of fog ... like he was of the fog ... like he was the fog. I didn't need to see him. His voice told me all I needed to know.

"Fuck you, Andrei."

"Tsk-tsk, my dear. You know how such language offends my delicate sensibilities."

"I don't give a *fuck*." I put a little extra on the "fuck," just to piss him off. "You're supposed to be dead."

"You know I can't die, and neither can you."

"You know what I mean. I drowned your ass. We can't deal with running water. Plus, that chain should have kept you pinned down there."

"Running water, my dear, sweet Elizabeth. Running being the operative word. I merely needed to wait out the authorities and cast that silly chain aside. You really should have tried harder, my dear. Much harder."

Andrei paced the roof as I kept a wary eye on him. Paced wasn't exactly right, was it? It was more like swirled and flowed with the fog, as if he were the fog. Huh. Maybe I hadn't brought the wrath of the marine layer down upon San Francisco like I had thought.

"Look, asshole, what do you want?"

"So you met my real estate agent?"

What? How in the hell did he know Sarah?

"Sarah?"

"She was tasty, that one. The only one in three hundred years to escape me ... "

Andrei drifted off into a thousand-yard stare at the streets below.

"Did you feed on her?"

"Quite regularly, in fact."

My interest was piqued; I needed to know more. But before I could pursue this line of questioning, Andrei offered a query of his own.

"Your detective friend not what he ... seemed?"

Andrei's accent thickened as he searched for the correct English words and phrases. His speech pattern and the question took me by surprise.

A pregnant pause. "No, but somehow I suspect you knew that."

He stared at the surface of the roof with his hands behind his back and drifted along back and forth in front of me. I hated this motherfucker with every fiber of my being, but I needed answers. Tolerating his presence was something I would just have to do.

"Ah, yes. You see, I didn't kill Detective Dietrich's grandfather, my dear."

"Oh? So he had it wrong, then? Had the wrong guy? Most killers proclaim their innocence, you know."

"Not quite. He didn't tell you ... how you say ... the whole truth. You see, Elizabeth, I killed Jonas Dietrich almost seventy years ago."

Well, wasn't that a kick in the head. I was stunned at first, but this revelation explained a lot.

"So, that's why he's been on your tail, trying to hunt you down? Trying to exact some measure of revenge?"

"Perhaps; perhaps not. I don't think he wanted to avenge himself. But, his wife and daughter ... maybe ... ?"

Andrei's voice turned playful and rose in pitch on those last five words from his pie hole. A coy, childlike expression transformed his face.

"You are a piece of work, Andrei, you know that? I know it was you who tormented me all those years. I know it was your face in the window. I know it was you in my bedroom all those years ago. What I want to know is ... why?"

"The time for ... share is over, yes?"

"Oh, so you're done sharing? How about I make you share?"

"I am older and stronger than you. You are but a baby, barely awake in your new world of darkness and blood."

"I bested you once … "

"Luck."

"What do you know about Serge Da Rocha?"

If a vampire's complexion could turn ashen, Andrei's did. He thrust his hands in his pockets and kicked at pebbles.

"Do not speak that name to me."

"Interesting. Seems I have a way of touching certain nerves with you."

"Y-y-you've seen him?"

This was the first time Andrei had stammered during any of our encounters. I was shocked.

"I have. Twice. And lived to tell the tale. Twice."

"Pray there won't be a third."

And with that, Andrei backpedaled deeper into the fog and vanished into the darkness beyond the wispy veil. I still had so many questions, but I did learn one thing about Andrei. He was scared, and I knew what he feared.

Serge Da Rocha.

I suppose I overplayed my hand a bit by dropping Da Rocha's name at that point in the conversation. Andrei had always gotten the drop on me, and he had done so again tonight. But I'd been able to turn the tables on him. I'd discovered a weakness, and I'd found out some things about my dear detective as well. My friend-murdering, lying bastard, dear detective. He and I were going to have a nice long chat, and soon. There was no way I was letting him off the hook for Whitney, and after what Andrei had just told me, Jonas Dietrich had some explaining to do.

I lingered on the roof for a good long while, ruminating on what I had learned this night. And Andrei ... that fucking guy and I were going to rumble. How in the hell had he survived the lagoon?

What more about my condition didn't I know? So many of the legends had turned out to be true, but still more were little more than the whims of fiction writers and Hollywood directors. I was almost trapped forever when I fell in the water. How in the world had Andrei gotten out of his watery grave?

I could become a bat. I hated sunlight. I needed living human blood to survive. I had the strength of ten men. I had World Class running speed. My anguish could bring thunder, lightning, and rain from the heavens. Religious iconography disturbed and weakened me. I knew an awful lot. So, what didn't I know? What was left?

Other troubling thoughts raced through my brain.

Sarah and Christina.

Sarah had escaped Andrei's clutches, but it wasn't like he couldn't find her. She was hiding in plain sight. High-profile real estate agent. So, why hadn't he finished her off? And Christina had had some kind of history with Dietrich, and I was pretty sure there was more to it that I had thought initially.

My nocturnal feeding habits hadn't been sexual in

nature until those two gorgeous, sexy women. Sure, I felt an orgasmic rush when I fed, when I took a life—some stronger than others depending on the quality of that life. But Sarah and Christina were different. I had never been attracted to women until those two. Now I knew why I was. Andrei and Jonas had left their residue on them, and it was like a magnet.

    I was extremely thirsty.

CHAPTER XXII

I arose from my unearthly slumber to find more critters in my chamber. My flight back to the church was a vague, faded memory, almost like falling asleep at the wheel. You wake up and have no idea how you got past the last five exits without plowing into the back of a semi. Whoa. Déjà vu.

I frantically searched for my sketchbook. Once I finally found it, I hastily drew Whitney, Andrei, and Dietrich all on one panel. The drawing looked like the cover of a dime store noir crime novel. Jonas hovering over a still-alive Whitney in the void between buildings, Andrei emerging out of the fog. I added myself as a bat silhouetted against the full moon. Just as I finished what would barely qualify as a Halloween window decoration ...

"Hello, Elizabeth."

A familiar voice. A friendly voice.

This shit really needed to stop. When was I going to get the drop on these guys instead of the other way around? Dietrich emerged from the shadows and rose from a cross-legged sitting position.

"How've you been?"

"Fuck you, Jonas."

"Yeah, I suppose I deserve that."

Deserve it? He deserved much more than that. He deserved a shovel to the face or a wooden stake in the heart. I was vulnerable, however, still seated in my coffin. Leverage, I did not have. Rapier-like wit, on the other hand…

"Oh, let's see … what do you deserve? A fate worse than death? Oh, wait … "

"Yep, that too. Bring it on. What else you got?"

"Goddammit, Jonas, you killed my friend."

"Oh. I didn't know you knew her."

"Yeah, well, I didn't know you were a lying, cocksucking bloodsucker."

"Well, when you put it that way, it sounds much, much worse."

"Fuck you." I spat the words at him.

"Look, I lied to you. I admit it. And I'm sorry. But I protected you. I ran interference for you. I blew my cover for you. I'm a fugitive because of all that. I should have told you from the beginning, but I thought I could get to Andrei by getting close to you."

"So, you used me? I wish I could be mad at you for that, but I was doing the same thing, using you to get to Andrei.

But that bullshit about your grandfather … really, Jonas. Explain it."

He wandered around the crypt, composing his thoughts, straining to remember the details. Dietrich spilled it and told me about his wife and daughter and the vampire who had murdered them. Jonas had been a detective in San Francisco in the 1940s, and Andrei had come to the window and peeped while Dietrich worked the night shift. Before long, the story sounded all too familiar and ended the way I thought it would. Andrei killed Jonas's family and turned him.

"Quite the brood you have here."

"Yeah, well, they just kind of showed up."

"Anyway, I vowed my revenge the night I awoke in my grave. The wood of the coffin broke easily, thanks to my newfound strength, and I dug my way out. I discovered my wife … and my daughter … were no more. I returned to the SFPD every generation and posed as a descendant of a long-dead detective. They bought it every time, and I have been working the odd cases ever since, and trying to end Andrei once and for all. I thought you'd ended him that night at Sutro Baths."

I still felt like he wasn't being honest, like he was lying and leaving out a lot of information. His story was tragic, and it certainly added fuel to the fire of my hatred for Andrei, but I couldn't help but think Jonas was keeping something from me. Never mind the fact that it finally dawned on me how Jonas knew about this place. He had once made this his sanctuary. I threw up in my mouth a little.

"Look, Jonas, while I can certainly empathize with you about your family ... and I hate Andrei as much as you do, and I can almost overlook your lies and coyness, I will never forgive you for Whitney. I read your note over and over, and it hurts me to think we could have fallen for each other. You're no better than he is."

That last sentence stung both of us. I wasn't sure I meant it, but Jonas needed to know that what he had done to me, to Whitney, was not okay. I would be damned if I was going to forgive him for Whitney.

"Wow."

Yeah, wow.

"I think you should go, Jonas."

"Now, wait a minute, Elizabeth, I think we should team up. Try to rid the world of Andrei once and for all. Something odd happened to him when he turned or became or whatever you call it. He's a pedophile. Maybe he was a pedophile before he became a vampire. All I know is that we need to do something about it."

A vampire pedophile. That was rich.

"*We* aren't going to do anything, Columbo. I thought we were a team, but you left me here to my own devices. Left me with more questions than answers. And what about Da Rocha? It's only a matter of time before that asshole shows up again. Your cover ... "

"Thanks to you—"

"What-the-fuck-ever, isn't helping us anymore. Your boy Tim and his pack of militarized dogs will be upon us before we know it. Between Andrei, you, Da Rocha, and your old cop buddies, I feel like I'm on an island, here. And right now, I need to think. You need to get out of my sight."

"Eliza—"

"GO!"

As Dietrich slunk back into the darkness, anger and sorrow welled up inside me. Or, worse yet, it was the thirst.

And oh, was I thirsty.

CHAPTER XXIII

You ever feel like you're being watched? Even when it is damn near impossible for anything, and I mean anything, to be watching you? I guess there's always a bigger fish or a more cunning predator.

My fifteen-minute flight to Golden Gate Park was uneventful, but I had this nagging feeling I was being watched the whole damn time. Even in my state as a bat, with all the sensory overload it entailed, this itch in my brain told me to be wary.

After regaining my form, I wandered the park for hours. The trails took me past the lawn bowling courts and the carousel, Robin Williams Meadow, and Hippie Hill. Small fires dotted the low rolling hills above the paved walkways as couples and trios and quartets played music, smoked pot and cigarettes, and drank liquor from bottles hidden inside crumpled brown paper bags. I almost caused a stampede when I strolled past the bison enclosure. I guess they don't care for the undead much.

Did I mention I was thirsty?

The pond where Whitney and I had sat was deserted. I felt a pang for her. I thought about trying to contact her folks, to tell them that they needn't worry anymore. Then I remembered what she had told me about them, and I figured they had stopped their worrying a long time ago.

Yellow police tape barred entry to the tunnel where I had fed. A chalk outline marked the spot where the bongo player ended; shards of the bongo still littered the ground around it. Feeding here again was probably a bad idea. I went deeper into the park, farther than I had ever been, either alive or dead. I was starting to give up hope, starting to think I would need to find another hunting ground, when I found them.

Just beyond a row of hedges up on a rise above a secluded pathway, a young couple, naked as the day they were born, fucked as if they were the last people on earth. Taking up a position in a nearby tree with all the stealth of a ninja, I watched them make love. Writhing in the wet grass, thrusting and moaning, her legs wrapped around his torso, his knees drawn up under her buttocks.

I licked my lips as I spied from my perch. A twinge of jealousy crept into my belly. I would never know this kind of passion again, not that I really had known it when I was alive. Oh, sure, I knew I could take penetration as before, but my new existence didn't allow for traditional sexual stimulation. Mine was ... different ... and I liked my way better. My way put me in control. And I liked being in control.

Just before the male climaxed, I leapt onto his back like a cowboy onto a rodeo bronco. Before he could buck me off, I sank my fangs into the side of his neck and tore open his jugular vein. His body stiffened, and he orgasmed and ejaculated as his blood began to flow into my hungry mouth. It took a moment for his mate to realize this had turned into a ménage a trois. Her head was on the opposite side of her lover's, and she didn't see me right away.

When she did, she let out a scream that could not be confused with the pleasures of the flesh or throes of passion. It was bloodcurdling. My weight was on top of her man, and her man's weight was on top of her, and she couldn't move. She was pinned to the ground, trapped while I feasted on her lover. His blood dripped onto her face and chest. She looked at me in horror.

"Don't worry, honey; you just have to wait your turn."

She fainted.

When I was finished with the male, I got up and rolled him off his woman. The odors were intoxicating. The smell of blood and semen and sex filled the crisp night air. Oh, how I wished I could actually breathe it in. I mimicked the act anyway.

I dropped to my knees, straddling the unconscious female. I slapped her across the face a few times until she came to. Placing my hand over her mouth, I said, "Scream, and I snap your neck. Blink twice if you understand." She blinked twice. Taking her in with all my senses, I knew I'd chosen wisely. She was young and voluptuous, very much a sexual creature. She just oozed sensuality despite her mortal fear. With my free hand, I raked my nails across her belly and breasts hard enough to the break the skin. She arched her back and moaned as I licked the blood from the scratches.

My tongue drew a straight line of blood residue from her navel to her throat. I licked the pulsing veins and arteries as they carried her life-giving blood to and from her brain. My mouth latched on. I bit down hard, my fangs piercing her supple skin and opening the flow of sweet nectar. I felt that familiar rush as her heartbeat began to slow from a rapid pounding to an intermittent thump-thump … thump—thump … thump—thump … thump.

I tipped my head back and let the pool of blood in my mouth slide down my esophagus, nourishing my unnatural existence, temporarily slaking my unquenchable thirst, and providing a release that nothing else could.

In my bloodlust, I was unaware of the approaching beat cops. I heard them before I saw them, but they saw me before I realized they were there.

"FREEZE!" The male of the pair shouted as they both drew their weapons and approached cautiously. Neither officer was athletic. The male had spent too much of his career in the donut shop, and the female was built like a truck. In my previous life, I could have outrun them, although I was pretty sure I couldn't outrun bullets in either state.

"On yer feet, hands where I can see 'em!"

I interlaced my fingers behind my head and rose.

"Turn around!"

"Barking at me isn't going to get you anywhere, Officer."

"I'm giving the orders here, miss."

"Suit yourself. Don't say I didn't warn you."

"Turn around, nice and slow," the female said as calmly as she could.

I did as I was told. Their jaws dropped simultaneously when they saw the blood on my face, neck, and chest.

"On the ground, g-g-g-get on the ground, now."

"No."

"Cuff her, Johansen," the male cop ordered.

"Me? You do it. I'm not touching this bitch."

As they bickered, I bolted.

"Oh, shit!" Johansen exclaimed.

My pursuers started shooting at me. Their aim was terrible, lucky for me. Either that, or I was just that elusive. I could hear them shouting into their walkie-talkies for backup. Although my speed allowed me to outpace them, I was still worried about catching a bullet or running into some of their compatriots. I found my way back to Robin Williams Meadow. At a full sprint, and with the two cops still on a wooded path, something *shifted*.

Instead of running on two legs, I was running on all

fours. My vision was different. My hearing even more acute and sensitive. My sense of smell was overwhelming. I looked down to see black legs and paws. I was a *wolf? What the* … ? I broke right up Hippie Hill and into the woods and stopped. I sat back on my haunches and watched the two cops in pursuit. They stopped in the middle of the meadow.

"Where the fuck did she go?" Johansen asked.

"No … idea … " too-many-donuts cop replied, all out of breath.

I brazenly emerged from my hiding spot. I wasn't dumb enough to give them reason to shoot at me, but I wanted them to see. I needed them to see.

"What the fuck is that, Johansen?"

"That's the biggest dog I've ever seen."

"That's no dog."

I turned and bolted up Hippie Hill into the trees before they thought to call Animal Control. Maybe they thought something had escaped from the San Francisco Zoo. Resisting the urge to sniff and pee on everything, I padded my way back to my sanctuary. I'd had enough excitement for one night.

It was a bit of a hike, and I was relieved when Blackfoot greeted me in the crypt. She knew me, even in this form. This strange, remarkable cat wound figure-eights between my legs as I calmed myself enough to become me again.

Another transformation, and I still had my clothes on. This time, I'd half-expected to be buck naked when I returned to normal. One thing I did know was these transformations were triggered by fight-or-flight responses. At least the first time. After the first flying experience, I'd wondered what else I could become. I had one answer, and after my latest encounter with Andrei, I thought there might be a few more possibilities.

Fog. Mist.

Now, that would be interesting.

I took my rest, thinking about all the things I might be able to morph into. What other creatures of the night did I even want to be? Bat and wolf were cliché, but they were also my reality. Could I command the denizens of my crypt? Could I make them do my bidding? When I saw through the bat's eyes the first time, I thought I might be able to. It *felt* like I might be able to.

I took off some of my clothing and cleaned up the best I could. My outfit had taken a beating the past few nights, and it was getting high time for a little shoplifting.

I closed my eyes and made a mental note that the next night would be time for experiments and a new wardrobe.

CHAPTER XXIV

When I awakened from my slumber and shook the cobwebs loose, I wasn't sure how I was going to make sense of everything, and I damn sure didn't know what I was going to do about any of it. There were two enemies that needed to go, Andrei and Serge Da Rocha.

And my dear detective ... what to do about you?

The things Dietrich and Andrei had told me about how things came to be and who was really who blew my mind. I was stunned by how coy and evasive Dietrich had been with me during each of our encounters. He really had tried to play me for a fool. He thought he could play dumb and get leads and information from me. He wouldn't have told me the truth about what he was or his history with Andrei if he didn't have to.

And what about Da Rocha? A sudden realization hit

me. He had to be hunting all three of us. I wondered if this little dark, twisted triangle struck him as funny, or if he were just a mechanism devoid of emotion and did his job without worrying about the back stories of the monsters he dispatched.

After ruminating on these things for a bit, I rose to meet the night. I took stock of the menagerie of roomies I had attracted. The colony of bats had grown quite large.

"Jeeezus Christ, there are a lot of you. Where in the hell did you all come from?"

My query was met with squeaks, squeals, and squawks, as if the flying mammals didn't care for my blasphemy or my curiosity. The colony stretched their collective wing membranes and flew through a hole in the roof. They were off to hunt, and I needed to do the same, lest another pair of lovers in the park meet the same fate as last night's lovemakers—I had my mind on other prey.

I flew back to Haight-Ashbury, avoiding Golden Gate Park this time. For some reason, I found myself on the roof of the hostel again. Maybe I was pining for Whitney. Maybe I was hoping to run into Andrei again. Maybe I just liked it. Runaways were on the menu tonight. Well, new age hippies, to be more precise. Young adult vagabonds who came to San Francisco searching for a lifestyle and an aesthetic long-since passed. You know the kind … kids whose clothes either came from a vintage clothing shop or belonged in one on consignment. Or something from Abercrombie and Fitch made to look worn. The guys rocking dear old dad's faded Army jacket, even though the kid had neither the constitution or the balls to enlist. Smoking weed and pretending to be hippies and railing against "the man" were preferable to serving the country.

The girls were either tagalongs or tragic, starving artists like Whitney. Their outfits might have looked good once, but now they were torn and dingy. Heads of hair hadn't seen shampoo in weeks or months, dirt had accumulated under fingernails and toenails, and the calloused soles of feet were visible through holes in their shoes.

My target for the night had future cult leader or politician written all over him. He had an aura about him. The other twenty-somethings and even the teenagers flocked to him as he held court on the stoop of the hostel. He wore a Navy peacoat and faded jeans. A black watch cap was loose and floppy on the back of his shaggy, unkempt hair. He wore a beard, but it wasn't too long or a five o'clock shadow, and it worked for him. It was a look I could almost dig, except for the God-awful sandals he wore.

He spoke of social justice and socialism and the greater good. He opined on corrupt cops and their mistreatment of people of color and how we all needed to do something about it. His passionate pleas found a willing audience at first, but when he tried to tell the kids the American dream as they knew it was a selfish fantasy, they tuned him out. And frankly, I couldn't wait for him to shut the fuck up. There was another existence beyond the veil, one he knew nothing about, that made his world look like Mr. Rogers' make-believe.

As his audience shrank, our friendly neighborhood social justice warrior resigned himself to pontificating on another night or perhaps to a different and more willing audience. He'd never get that chance.

The discouraged would-be activist thrust his hands in his pockets and wandered off in search of revolutionaries, kindred spirits, or spirits of another kind. I leapt rooftop to rooftop to get ahead of him and dropped down into an alley. Jumping two or three stories with no ill effects still mystified me, even though I knew I had some extraordinary abilities.

"Hey, you."

The would-be activist or cult leader glanced in my direction into the alley, but he was determined to keep walking.

"Pssssssst. C'mere."

He stopped in front of the alley and looked around with a *who, me?* look on his face.

What a spy movie cliché I was, but it was fun. I didn't take enough pleasure in these moments. Oh, sure, the kills were orgasmic, but this part, the buildup, the stalking ... I rarely did because my prey were usually targets of opportunity, animalistic rather than ritualistic. Andrei's kills were calculated. I still hadn't developed an MO, or even a technique. He savored the moments before, the hours before, maybe even the days before. For me, it was a chase and kill as if I had turned San Francisco into the Serengeti. Hell, even lionesses stalked in the long grass before pouncing.

Well, whether it be bound torture or track down and kill, I needed to learn how to be subtle and nuanced. This was my way of life now. I wouldn't get very far by continuing to kill and leave my victims for anyone to find. I wasn't paranoid by nature, but I could feel the squeeze of law enforcement all around me getting tighter each night. Every patrol car or ambulance or fire engine ... any vehicle with lights on the roof, really ... caused me to panic a little. Fluttering around town on bat wings had kept me off the radar while in transit to and from my hideaway, but my kills, with the exception of the musicians I had stashed in North Beach, were way too public. And I was about to do it again.

"Yeah, you. C'mere. I want to help you."

His sandals made that cliched *clip-clip* sound as he strolled toward me nonchalantly. His hands were still buried in his pockets, and his eyes never left the ground until I stepped out of the shadows.

"Who are you?"

"I want to help you. I heard you talking. I liked what you had to say."

I circled him like a shark as I purred and cooed.

"That's great, but you're creeping me out, lady."

"You're cute." I turned on my best smolder. At least I thought it was smolder.

He tried to turn his head away as I got in his face. My eyes made contact with his in a missile lock, and he froze. My wannabe politician was a bit taller than me, even in my boot heels, and I had to look up at him. That just put his throat at a convenient biting height. I pulled open his peacoat, grabbed him by his stubble-covered chin, and turned his head to my left. I ran my tongue from the opening in his button-down shirt all the way to the cut of his jaw. I kissed his neck and nibbled on his earlobe. "Fuck this."

As the " ... this" left my lips, my meal snapped out of his trance and shoved me backward, hard. I took three fast steps and tackled him with a guttural growl.

"Please, no ... don't hurt me ... "

I tipped my head back and bared my fangs.

"W-w-w-what are you?"

My answer was to grab him by the face and yank his head to the side. I brought my fangs to bear hard and swift. There was an audible popping sound like a good hotdog casing as the tips pierced his flesh and brought the river of hot blood flowing into my mouth.

He tried to push me away, but the more I sucked, the weaker he got, and I had leverage. I did take my time with this part, though. Oh, did I ever. And it was glorious ... the gradual slowing of his heartbeat, the twitching, the shallow breathing. It all drew down as his blood nourished me and recharged me. His expiration gave me a jolt of energy.

Ever since the poor, disgruntled salesman, I was keenly aware of the effect the blood of different types of people had on me. Failures in life were to be avoided. The young and virile were preferable. The extremely young were even better, but I had sworn off children. Ever since I'd woken up with that poor little girl in my arms, children were off the menu. I had kinda broken that self-imposed rule with Billy's sister and the street kids who had stolen Whitney's stuff. But those little punks had deserved it.

A thought popped into my head that elicited actual laughter. I could become that avenging angel I'd thought was so silly just a few weeks ago. Could you imagine? Me? Vampire vigilante? Cleaning up the streets of San Francisco and ridding the neighborhoods of ne'er-do-wells? Hunter's Point and the Tenderloin would be safe to walk at night within a week. The thought was laughable.

My chortling was interrupted by the sight of a familiar hulking figure at the mouth of the alley. *Da Rocha.* "Bastard." As energized as I was from my feeding, I was in no mood for a fight with this brute. He was always prepared, and I was always caught unaware. I turned and sprinted, transforming into a bat as I reached top speed before I exited the alley. Da Rocha pulled out a weapon and fired. Before I could climb to a safe altitude, I was ensnared in a net. I crashed into a cinder block wall and landed on top of a corral of metal garbage cans.

Da Rocha reeled me in like I was a game fish as I transformed back into my human form against my will. Despite my incredible strength, I could not break free from this net.

"Stop struggling, Elizabeth. Better not to struggle."

Da Rocha's Portuguese accent was heavy, but his English was clear and well enunciated. I wasn't sure why this had jumped out at me, nor did I know what to expect, since this was the first time I'd heard the man speak. And I wasn't surprised he knew my name, either. It was odd hearing it come out of his face, but he wouldn't have been worth his salt if he didn't understand his prey.

He dragged me down the alley, scooped me up, and tossed me in the back of a waiting black SUV. I could have escaped the vehicle easily, but the net confounded me. I didn't know how it could be so strong, and I didn't understand why I couldn't break it. Tools of the international vampire-hunting trade, I surmised.

The next fifteen minutes were agonizing. I knew who had me, so small talk or taunting weren't going to work. I wasn't going to be able to charm or sarcasm my way out of this one. Although time slowed to a crawl, I wouldn't have to wait too long to learn our destination.

St. Paul's Church.

Now I knew who had commissioned Da Rocha's services: the San Francisco Catholic Archdiocese. Was I the only target, or was he also after Dietrich and Andrei? Were there other vampires in The City?

Da Rocha parked the SUV at the back of the church. He threw open the back end and hauled me out of it unceremoniously. Da Rocha didn't really care that he was causing road rash and tearing up my outfit. I was really going to need new clothes if I survived this.

The vampire hunter extraordinaire dragged me to the altar where a slab of a table and a priest awaited. The priest wore ceremonial garb. Candles burned on either side of the pulpit and cast dancing shadows on the floor and walls.

The priest chanted incantations in Latin as Da Rocha hoisted me onto the table. My presence in a church on consecrated ground weakened me. I was no match for Da Rocha as he freed me from the net and bound me to the slab with leather straps on my wrists and ankles. The garlic that decorated the place didn't help much, either.

A stake, a mallet, and a broadsword sat atop a small stand nearby.

"What are those for?"

"After we stake you, we cut off your head and take out your heart."

"Oh, lovely. I think I'll pass."

"You have no choice. We must end you. You are unnatural. You are evil. We must save your soul."

"Who the fuck are you to judge? You don't know me! You don't know what's in my heart. And I don't have a soul to save."

"That's why we have him."

Da Rocha tossed his head toward the priest, who was still reading incantations and crossing himself and us. "I command you, unclean spirit, whoever you are ... *blah, blah, blah.*" The priest picked up a decanter and shook it at me, expelling a liquid. The holy water hit my skin and burned instantly. The searing pain was the most intense I had ever experienced.

I screamed.

My cries reverberated throughout the cathedral. I hadn't been scared until this very moment. When that holy water splashed me, the possibility that these men had the ability and the means to destroy me finally hit home.

As the priest continued to drone on in his monotone readings of what could only be the Roman Rituals and the Rites of Exorcism, he moved to put his hand on my forehead while Da Rocha made a move for the mallet and the pinpoint sharp stake. He stood over me with the stake in his left hand and the mallet in his right.

"The Lord be with you."

"And also with you."

I closed my eyes and let my thoughts drift. I wasn't going to let them see any more panic or fear. I hoped a solution to my dilemma would present itself; maybe my subconscious would rise to the occasion. My sanctuary appeared in my mind, and I could see the colony of bats in the rafters. Focusing my attention on the bats, I tried to get their attention telepathically. I didn't know if my abilities had a range, but we were sure as hell going to find out. Something *shifted*. The colony grew restless and all of a sudden took flight.

The route between St. Paul's and my sanctuary showed itself as I tried to serve as a GPS for the bats. Da Rocha and the priest stopped what they were doing and craned their necks to listen as hundreds of bats descended upon the church. The bats flew in any way they could, through the bell tower and the HVAC system's ductwork.

Bats covered the iconography and swirled around my

would-be murderers. I felt a sudden rush of strength as the crucifix was obscured, and I broke the leather bonds at my wrists. More and more bats poured in and surrounded the clergyman and the vampire hunter.

I fussed with the straps at my ankles and finally freed myself. Standing on top of the table, I spread my arms wide and willed my charges to attack. Neither man spoke or called out. They just waved frantically at the horde. Da Rocha tried to pull the other man away, but the bats had him down on the floor. Within seconds the priest was covered with bite wounds, and blood oozed through the holes in his robes.

The priest's hand slipped out of Da Rocha's grasp as the bats overwhelmed him. I turned my attention to the church's top slayer and focused the bats on him. Da Rocha made for a vestibule and disappeared from my sight.

After I was convinced Da Rocha wasn't coming back for Round 2, I strutted out of the church. I pounded the floor, leaving burning footprints in my wake. Oh, did that make me happy. A devilish grin curled my lips as I burst through the double doors of the church and stepped out into the San Francisco night. I spun on a heel and flipped the building a double-bird as my bats disappeared into the cool late summer sky, silhouetting themselves against the moon.

"Fuck you."

I walked back to my sanctuary. There wasn't much time until sunrise, but there was enough, and I needed time to think and unwind. A good decompressing walk was what I needed, not a quick flight. Unfortunately, I didn't realize I was being followed.

The stroll was uneventful. Occasionally, I looked up to see my colony of bats, my squadron, providing air cover. It was a beautiful sight. So was my coffin. Boy, had I experienced the highs and lows of a vampiric existence on this night. From a beautiful feeding to a near-death experience, it was a bit much.

The colony returned to the rafters and cleaned the blood from each other's fur as they settled in for the day.

I thankfully found solace in my sarcophagus, and Blackfoot had probably sensed I needed a cuddle. She crawled in with me as I pulled the stone lid closed. I was done with this night, and I hoped it was done with me.

CHAPTER XXV

P anic. This was a sensation I hadn't felt since the morgue drawer. Anxiety and panic attacks I knew from the days when Andrei had haunted my waking nightmares. Years of therapy and immersion in school and work eventually mitigated the effects.

I arose from my unnatural slumber in a panic. If I could breathe, I would have been hyperventilating. If my heart could beat, it would have been thumping out of my chest. My palms would have been sweaty. My armpits and feet would have stunk.

This was an entirely new experience. All the physiological signs of a panic attack were present, except for the accompanying bodily reflexes that just didn't exist anymore.

It was remarkable how calm I had been during the ordeal of the night before. I'd struggled against the net, but once I'd realized it was stronger than me, I'd quit fighting it.

Once I'd gone away and found my colony telepathically, the solution had presented itself. I wasn't sure if I could command these creatures on demand or transform whenever I willed it. These events only happened when I was in mortal danger, except that after the first time I became a bat because I had to, I was able to do so whenever I wanted to. I wondered if the wolf would come if I called. I wondered if I could become fog or mist like Andrei. That was a trick I hadn't tried yet.

After I'd pushed aside the stone cap, Blackfoot leapt out and ran off to do Blackfoot things, while I was left to ponder the events of the past few days. Every night was a harrowing adventure since Dietrich had murdered my friend. This trio of men in my life was as eclectic as it gets. Pacing my safe space, I thought about these three idiots: the detective, the vampire slayer, and the asshole vampire.

It stung when I thought about my last conversation with Dietrich. I should have taken the opportunity to pick his brain and guilt him into telling me everything about everything. But I was so angry about his lies and what I perceived to be betrayal that I just couldn't stand to be in his presence. And Andrei … well, fuck him.

Da Rocha.

He was the clear and present danger. He was the one who was actively hunting me. He was the one who had tried to end me, thrice. He was the one who had to go.

But what to do, what to do?

I had no way to know where he was or who he was associating with. What I did know was that I needed to go on the offensive. I had spent too much time playing defense and warding off unannounced ambush attacks from a trained assassin. This was just going to get me killed, or worse.

Maybe I could go back to St. Paul's. See if Da Rocha had gone back there to check on the fate of the priest. Perpetrators often went back to the scene of the crime, no? Why wouldn't Da Rocha go back to the people who'd hired him to dispatch me? Maybe he was meeting with the Archbishop or other high-ranking diocese officials to discuss ways to deal with the shape-shifting vampire with telepathic command of a colony of bats.

Well, if I didn't get struck with a bolt-of-lightning idea.

Wandering around the streets of San Francisco was too dangerous and counterproductive. There was too much ground to cover and not enough time to cover it. I had been lucky so far that Da Rocha hadn't found my sanctuary, and I had been here longer than any other hiding place I had found.

It made me sick to know that Dietrich the vampire detective had used it as his refuge, and that he'd kept this information from me. And the idiot I am just blindly followed along, never questioning how he knew about this place, never asking where all the church trappings and accoutrements went or who had removed them.

It was comforting to know I had found a few other strategic locations to bugger off to if I had to. I had a feeling

I was going to have to use one or two before I was done with Serge Da Rocha.

As for my bolt-of-lightning idea? Yeah, that.

I climbed to the roof of the abandoned church and looked to the overcast summer San Francisco sky. Fall was coming. I could feel it in my bones. This made me happy. Communing with my colony to send them out into the night to find Da Rocha? Well, that made me downright giddy. I cackled like a witch as my minions took to the air and spread out across the city. As they reached altitude, something *shifted*.

The bats were on a reconnaissance mission of the highest priority. Da Rocha must be found at all costs and dealt with accordingly. He had gotten the drop on me three times, and I was going to turn the tables on him. There was no way I was going to be able to address things with the other two if Da Rocha kept popping up when I least expected it. Hell, he was already cramping my style when it came to my feeding habits. And that wouldn't do; not at all.

I saw as the bats saw, as if I were watching a bank of televisions at Walmart or Best Buy. Except instead of catching the game or watching endless loops of demo programming, I saw sweeping views of skyscrapers and apartment buildings, churches and restaurants, pizza parlors and panoramic views of the bay and the bridges as my charges searched high and low for their—my—quarry.

I summoned every manner of nocturnal creature that would heed my call. Insects of indeterminate species, rats, mice, spiders, crows, owls, turkey vultures ... you name it. The raging headache threatened to split my skull as my brain was overloaded with information. I wasn't getting just visuals, I was getting sound, too.

The cacophony of sounds was hard to wade through at first, but with a little practice and concentration I was able to put together a three-hundred-and-sixty-degree experience and take it all in, the audio and visuals, like a preternatural theater in the round.

My head turned reflexively, and I craned my neck involuntarily as I tried to process the incoming information. Certain views and sounds would catch my attention, but I quickly learned what data to discard and what to focus on. I directed my minions to the churches in the area, notably ones with rectories. Da Rocha was likely to be staying at one. He may have been a mercenary, but he was also a servant of God, a soldier for God ... for all gods. He'd stay close to his meal ticket.

After several hours of searching, and wiping my nose Lord knows how many times, thanks to a recurring nosebleed or whatever it was, I was getting ready to give up for the night. The airborne creatures fanned out from the interior of The City and skirted the coast.

What a squadron of bats found at Crissy Field would have taken my breath away if I could breathe.

Jonas Dietrich and Serge Da Rocha were trading haymakers on a sandy strip of nasty beach just north of the field, and Dietrich was getting the worst of it. I never could imagine Jonas taking part in the more rigorous aspects of police work, like chasing down bad guys or getting physical with suspects. He didn't strike me as a pugilist. I, not Jonas, had taken Andrei on at Sutro Baths. The fight continued as Da Rocha backed Dietrich into a construction zone. Dietrich grabbed a two-by-four and struck a glancing blow off the hunter's shoulder. Da Rocha may have been human, but he was more than a match for the meek detective, vampire or not.

Regardless of how things had shaken out with Dietrich, as angry I was with him, as betrayed as I felt, I had feelings for him. I thought of his note and how he'd ended it. I couldn't leave him in the hands of Da Rocha. The slayer would end him if I didn't intervene. As I willed myself into a transformation, I urged the squadron of bats to enter the fray as I mentally released the rest of my reconnaissance teams. My telepathic connection to them had weakened me, and I didn't need any unnecessary information flooding my neural network.

I took flight and made a beeline for Crissy Field. Flying as fast as I could, I tried to maintain my connection with the squadron of bats who were now circling Da Rocha. I just hoped I wasn't too late.

When I arrived on the scene, the squadron of bats was keeping Da Rocha busy while Dietrich licked his wounds and tried to find cover. The bats had suffered some casualties, and I felt the anguish of each of their deaths as they passed. It sharpened my resolve and steeled my nerves. Da

Rocha was going to be the end of me if I didn't do something about him. He'd eventually get around to Andrei, and as much as that was a tantalizing thought, I wanted the pleasure of doing it myself. Right now, Da Rocha was going to finish Dietrich off, and that just wouldn't do.

Da Rocha was taking damage from bat bites and tried to fend them off with wild, frantic arm swinging. I forced my transformation as I landed in a full-on strut and made my way toward the fracas.

"It ends now, Da Rocha! Leave him alone!"

My bats—MY bats! —created a veritable tornado around the slayer. They parted and allowed me to pass through. It was heady stuff, having an airwing at my command. My power was growing at a startling rate, a fact confirmed by the look on Da Rocha's face. He was in shock and awed by my abilities.

"This is not possible. Never have I seen this before."

"No? You ain't seen nothing yet, sweetness."

I stopped a few feet in front of him and sized him up.

"Jonas happens to be a friend of mine. I don't take too kindly to people hurting my friends. Frankly, I'm sick of you showing up unannounced and trying to hurt me, too. That little ambush with the net gun and your special guest star at the church? I didn't appreciate any of that."

"You are evil. You are vampire. You must be destroyed."

"Yeah, see, you keep saying that. I don't appreciate that none too much, either."

Da Rocha spit at the ground in front of my feet and

looked up at me with malice in his eyes. I hauled off and hit him square in the jaw with a right hook that surprised us both. The blow dislocated the jaw and knocked him to the ground. He popped his mandible back into place with a grimace and a grunt. Da Rocha glared at me from one knee as he debated his next move and rubbed his injured face.

As Da Rocha got to his feet, Dietrich jumped off a piece of construction equipment, wielding a two-by-four. He brought the piece of wood down hard on the back of the slayer's head with what was meant to be a killing blow. Da Rocha went face first into the sand, but after a slight pause, he pushed himself up and rolled to one side, barely eluding another head-smasher from Jonas.

Da Rocha sprang to his feet and confronted the two of us. His arms hung at his sides, his hands balled into fists. His knuckles cracked and he seethed with rage.

Jonas shot me a nervous glance.

"I never really was much of a fighter."

"Ya think? You better become one quick, or it'll be curtains for us, Detective."

"Yeah, well, I never really had much of a reason—"

"Oh? A San Francisco cop who never had to get physical? That's rich, Jonas."

In a low growl, Da Rocha rumbled, "Will you two be quiet?"

A fog bank kicked up out of nowhere and started to roll in off the water toward us on the beach. Andrei materialized out of the mist, stepped onto terra firma, and strolled toward us.

"Oh, for fuck's sake."

"Language, *Elizabeth*."

"What the hell are you doing here?"

"Easy, *Detective*. We have a ... how you say ... common enemy. The enemy of my enemy is my friend, no?"

"I don't think so, asshole. You can go fuck yourself."

Andrei cringed at my use of profanity. He actually looked pained just hearing the words come out of my mouth. My foul mouth and Andrei's disdain for it were the least of my worries right now. The three men in my life, for better or for worse, were within shouting distance, and the two I needed to end were within striking distance.

"Seriously, Andrei, what are you doing here?"

"Well, my dear, our Mr. Da Rocha here has become a thorn in all our sides, it seems. Personally, I am not ready to be dispatched by him or his *ilk*." He spat the word and spit on the sand in front of the vampire hunter. "Isn't that correct, *slayer*?"

"You are all going to be destroyed. If not by my hand—"

Andrei let out a big belly laugh that caught me by surprise. His mannerisms were always so ... reserved, and he was always so ... sophisticated, or at least he pretended to be. I almost expected his accent to slip, but it didn't.

"Your indignation is laughable, my friend. You are in no position to make threats."

I was vaguely aware that Dietrich, Andrei, and I had started to circle Da Rocha; Dietrich only reluctantly so, at a slower pace, in fact, almost reticent.

"Get your shit together, Jonas."

"What are we doing, Elizabeth?"

"We're about to solve a problem."

"I'm a cop."

"No, you were a cop. You are now a fugitive. After this, there will be no going back. You won't be able to time hop your way through a career as a policeman anymore."

"Well, whose fault is that?"

"Oh, we're going to get petty now? I'm sorry about Christina. I really am. I couldn't help myself. Besides, you're the one who *tainted* her. Oh, yeah, I've been figuring some shit out. I'm hopelessly attracted to whomever one of you fuckers bites. You're going to start judging me now? Christina's on you. You shouldn't have taken me there. You killed my friend, so get with the program. This is happening."

The program, as it were, involved ridding ourselves of this pesky vampire hunter. We had the advantage. We had an overwhelming advantage. Three vampires against one human? He might have been an extraordinary human being, highly skilled and trained, but we had speed, strength, and ravenous appetites on our side.

What I didn't quite understand was Jonas's hesitation. Maybe it was Andrei's sudden appearance that set him off. This was the vampire who had turned him. This was the vampire who had murdered his family. This was the vampire he had tracked for more than half a century. Maybe the thought of a team-up was too off-putting for him.

"Seriously, Jonas, what the fuck is your problem?"

"Language, *Elizabeth*."

"Shut the fuck up, Andrei." I couldn't even stand to hear him utter my name.

"I don't know. Do we have to kill him?"

"You've obviously run into him before. You knew all about him. You had a file on him. He's not going away, Jonas. He's going to hunt us down one by one and end us. It doesn't matter where we go or where we try to hide. And you know what? I'm not averse to sending a little message to the Catholic church. We are not to be trifled with."

"What about him?" Jonas jerked his head in Andrei's direction.

"I agree, he's gotta go. We'll deal with him another day … er … night. Da Rocha is our immediate concern."

While we were bantering, Andrei picked up a piece of rebar and took a swing at the backs of Da Rocha's knees. The slayer dropped to his knees in pain and let out a howl.

"Do what you will. My soul has been saved. I will be welcomed into the house of the Lord. I will sit with God. I will live in paradise for all eternity. You are all damned to Hell."

"Tsk-tsk-tsk. We are forever, *mon ami*."

"French now, Andrei? Really? You really are a pretentious asshole."

My words seemed to enrage Andrei, and he took a swing at the back of Da Rocha's head. The hunter closed his eyes as if he knew it was coming. The blow landed at the base of the skull as if Andrei was swinging for McCovey Cove. Da Rocha went face first into the sand with a soft thud.

I flipped him over and dragged him over to a stack of wooden pylons.

"C'mon, Jonas, grab that rope."

Dietrich was stunned, but my words snapped him out of his funk. He hesitated at first, but he eventually grabbed a length of rope and handed it to me. I paused a moment as Andrei and I lashed Da Rocha to the beams.

"You like this, don't you, you *freak?*"

"Not now, my dear. Now is not the time," Andrei said flatly as he expertly bound Da Rocha's arms. It was truly macabre watching him work the ropes like he had hundreds of times before, including when he did it to me.

But he was right; it wasn't the time. We had bigger fish to fry. I couldn't forget waking up trussed on that wooden X in that abandoned loft with laughing boy leering at me. He strapped Da Rocha to the beams like a seasoned sailor. There was no way Da Rocha was getting out of this. Dietrich helped me tie off the slayer's legs. Da Rocha was splayed out like he was being crucified. We tied him and propped him with his back arched, pressure applied to key joints. Andrei secured the knots in such a way that the ropes would get tighter the more Da Rocha struggled ... if he had the chance to struggle. *Plenty of practice.*

"Grab that bucket, my boy."

"A British accent, Andrei? Really?"

"I'm a bit of a chameleon, my dear."

"You're something, all right."

Dietrich handed Andrei a bucket of putrid water, and Andrei splashed the entire contents in Da Rocha's face. The slayer spat the water out his mouth and blew it out of his nose in one large exhalation. The cocktail of construction site water and snot sprayed straight up and then headed downward, landing across his chambray shirt and leather vest.

Jonas wrapped his arms around himself and tried to disappear inside his raincoat.

"What's the matter, Detective? Squeamish?" Andrei asked.

"You weren't squeamish when you killed Whitney."

"For fuck's sake, would the two of you shut the fuck up? You should just fuck and get it over with. Godammit." Finally, some fire from Dietrich.

Jonas threw off his trench coat, revealing a physique I didn't know he possessed. A chiseled chest, flat stomach, rippling biceps ... and he *flew* to Da Rocha. Before the slayer could utter a word in protest, the detective tore open an artery in Da Rocha's throat. Blood sprayed in the air like a busted sprinkler head.

Andrei and I joined in as we ripped holes in major blood vessels and slaked our collective thirst on the blood of a vampire slayer. There was something so satisfying about taking Da Rocha's life. The syrupy red liquid was electrified with an energy I had yet to experience during any previous kill.

We took turns feeding on our would-be destroyer, this God-fearing, God-serving, trained vampire killer. I wanted to be the one to finish him off, to be the one to suck the last drops of blood from his dying body, to be the one who felt the final quiver, to be the one who stole the last breath, to be the one who experienced the last heartbeat. And I almost had to fight Andrei to do it. I would have done it gladly —*Ass!*—but he relented. Dietrich just wandered off, sick of the whole scene.

Andrei stumbled backward, drunk off the slayer's blood, as I moved in for the kill. Da Rocha, with the little strength he had left, reached up, grabbed the hair on top on my head, and pulled me close to his mouth.

"Hear me, you bitch of the devil," he hissed. "You will burn in Hell. The almighty God, our Lord in Hea—"

And that was the end of him. I didn't let him utter another word, not another syllable. He let out one final, raspy gasp as his heartbeat slowed and finally stopped. I savored and relished that final beat, almost hoping for one more, as his heart pushed the last of the crimson nectar into my waiting mouth and down my aching throat.

I sucked at the wound in his neck until I felt the blood vessels collapsing like a failed straw when there is no more liquid at the bottom of the container. I shuddered and twitched, a fire burned in my loins, and one last quiver wracked my body as electric shocks of preternatural energy sizzled along my nerves and into my brain.

I rose to my full height, wiped my mouth on my sleeve, and turned to face Andrei.

"*Elizabeth*, your eyes … "

"What about them, jackass?"

My voice wasn't quite my voice. It had taken on an otherworldly quality, almost as if I were speaking into an electronic voice changer. But this wasn't artificial, it emanated from within, deep within me, and my new dulcet tones rumbled up from my diaphragm through my trachea, over the vocal fold, and out of my mouth.

"They're, they're so … *blue*."

"Well, *Andrei*, you must be colorblind. I have green eyes."

"No, my dear, they're positively glowing blue … electric blue."

I knew about the red. I had seen Andrei's and Jonas' eyes in the act of feeding. But glowing blue? This was new. Andrei was fascinated and mortified at the same time. I really wished I could see myself in a mirror now. By the time I'd summoned a bat to commune with, the effect might wear off. It had to be related to the kill, or maybe even to whom I killed.

"Detective, come have a look, see for yourself."

"I don't wa … "

"Come now, see what our beloved *Elizabeth* has become!"

Jonas reluctantly crossed the ground between us. After

staring at the sand for several seconds, he finally looked up. His gaze met mine.

A look of sheer terror came over his face. His eyes widened. His jaw dropped. His mouth gaped wide.

"What?"

"Yo-yo-your eyes … "

"Yes, Jonas, we've established that."

"I've never seen anything like it. It's demonic."

"Well, aren't we being a little over-dramatic?"

Andrei burst into maniacal laughter and fell to the ground. He was rolling around, hugging himself as he giggled himself silly. Jonas was the first of us to hear the helicopter.

A police chopper was bearing down on our location, its searchlight sweeping the beach just east of our location. It would be on us in minutes.

"Time to go," Dietrich said in a flat monotone as if a police helicopter swooping in to get him was routine.

"I tend to agree, Jonas." There was a bit more urgency in my voice. I hesitated in saying anything to laughing boy, but I felt I owed him just a little something after our little vampiric team-up.

"ANDREI!" The chopper was getting loud. I jerked my thumb in the general direction of the whirlybird. "We gotta go!"

My stalker, my tormentor, my maker, got ahold of himself long enough to assess the situation and nod his understanding. We all agreed we needed to meet at another time and location. There was no time or opportunity to hide Da Rocha's exsanguinated corpse.

"Three nights from now, The Dark Truth, midnight," I spit out with as much confidence as I could muster. We needed a cooling off period after this.

"If you insist, my dear," Andrei said, matter-of-factly.

Jonas just nodded in the affirmative.

We took off in three different directions: Andrei to the south, Jonas west, and I went southwest. We didn't bump into each other, trying to decide which way to go, it was natural and instinctive. The buffeting of the helicopter's rotors was distracting and deafening as I took off running and initiated my transformation. It took a bit for me to get my bearings and orient myself to the proper vector for the flight back to my sanctuary. I frankly didn't give a damn about my co-conspirators. I should have cared about Jonas's plight, I should have worried about where he would seek refuge, I should've offered mine, but I didn't.

As for Andrei … well … he could go fuck himself, for all I cared.

When I returned to my abandoned church, I descended the rickety wooden stairs to the crypt. By gesture alone, I summoned my creatures. All manner of nocturnal beast came unto me, feral mammals, insects, arachnids … all. My outstretched arms were soon adorned with every manner of creepy crawlies. My feet and legs were encircled by rats, mice, opossums. The colony of bats flew around the space in squadrons and made figure eights around their queen.

I pet them, stroked them, scratched them. My electric blue eyes reflected in their animal eyeshine and radiated off their fur. Satisfied and reassured, they retreated to the cracks and the crevices and the nooks and crannies and the rafters.

This had to be the most eventful night since the becoming, since I'd woken up in that morgue drawer, dead, undead. My enemy, my mortal arch-enemy, had been dispatched. There would be no more sneak attacks from Serge Da Rocha. I had gone on the offensive, I had taken the fight to him, and I had emerged victorious. It almost made up for not winning Public Relations Professional of the Year.

Almost.

An eerie blue glow illuminated the interior of my sarcophagus as I pulled the stone cap back into place and bedded down for the day. I basked in it for a while as I waited for sleep to take me.

CHAPTER XXVI

What was I, really? Both Da Rocha and Andrei were stunned at the things they saw when it came to me. My glowing blue eyes. My command of the children of the night. The transformations hadn't fazed Da Rocha one bit, but these other two revelations were new experiences for him. I was pretty sure he had seen it all. The list of vampire—dare I utter the word—species he had encountered and dispatched was extensive. Surely, he had come across the likes of me before ... but apparently not.

Jonas, well, Jonas, on the other hand ... I was still trying to wrap my head around his conscientious-objector status when it came to offing a vampire hunter who wanted to end us. The only thing I could think of was his humanity. Jonas was still hanging onto it, or at least trying to. The facade of playing detective, reinventing himself as a descendant, cajoling members of the police force to give him the hours he wanted, to work the cases he wanted … the elements were staggering.

And Andrei. Tsk, tsk, tsk. I swear. What the hell was I going to do about him? I still didn't know anything about him. Sure, I had Jonas's information sheet, and I was pretty sure he was a pervert. That thought led me to another one. Did we vampires "become" differently? Did each one of us take on unique characteristics when we died and came back? I could become a bat or a wolf, Andrei could become mist, and Jonas was bereft of fighting spirit. Andrei saw things about me now he had never seen before, and he was the one who had turned me. He preyed on children, and I found the thought of hurting them abhorrent, so apparently, I didn't inherit any of his child-molesting tendencies.

But I was different. I knew it. I could feel it. Andrei's and Da Rocha's reactions to me proved it. I was going to get answers at this meeting, but it was still two days away. I wasn't sure what else I wanted to get out of it. There was an uneasy truce between the three of us. What a disturbing satanic triangle this had become.

Despite learning or confirming a great many things, there were so many things I still didn't know. Running water, religious iconography, OCD and counting, shape-shifting—all true. I hadn't put sunlight to the test, and deep down I knew it would be a mistake to tempt fate on that one. But why could I commune with night creatures, and what the hell was the deal with my electric blue eyes? Why was killing orgasmic for me? Why did I have a different experience with each victim? How did you even "make" a vampire?

Healing was a revelation. I had been shot and involved in numerous scuffles. My wounds and injuries healed at such a pace that I rarely remembered getting hurt in the first place. Well, I remembered my father shooting me in the stomach like it was five minutes ago, but not because of the gunshot wound. I rubbed my belly absentmindedly. I didn't recall much else from that night, and certainly not what I had done. Julie had to fill me in on that.

That was something else I didn't get. Why didn't I remember some of my kills? And why did I remember the rest like they'd just happened? I had no recollection of most of the events surrounding Steve's demise. I didn't even remember going to his apartment. Killing him was a different story. But the blackout surrounding my parents and the little girl? My intuition told me it had to do with how close I was to my victims. But that didn't make sense, because I didn't know Emily. That one, I chalked up to her young age.

None of it made any sense.

Was I done evolving now, or were there more changes to come? The way Andrei and Jonas had reacted, I had a feeling they couldn't tell me a damn thing about what was going on with myself.

CHAPTER XXVII

For the death of me, I would never understand why human beings, especially those who should know better, try to take on vampires after sundown. But maybe that's what I get for having a lie-in.

My cryptmates were better than any home alarm system on the planet. Their animal senses were still greater than mine, despite my advanced abilities. They heard the SWAT team long before I did. You'd think these cops in paramilitary gear would learn the art of stealth. But Jonas's old cop pal Tim was a bit of a blunt instrument, and he ran these raids like he was commanding a squad of storm troopers instead of a strategic, tactical team. Maybe they wanted payback for what I had done at Tunnel Top. Maybe they were upset over what had happened with Dietrich. Maybe they were too stupid to know any better.

What I did know was that Tim and the boys were

having a fuck of a time with the critters in the cathedral and the antechamber. They were causing such a commotion that I thought they would come through the ceiling and fall on my head. I was relieved to find I wasn't accompanied by a blue glow when I emerged from my vault, yet I was slightly disappointed. The other thing I knew was that I needed to get the hell out of there.

While my crack anti-home-invasion squad was giving the SWAT team fits, I made a mental note to wreck as much of the evidence of my machinations as I could. There was no way I would let these fools figure out where my hiding places were, but I couldn't go without my stuff. After pushing off the heavy stone lid with a mighty shove, *of course*, the cap cracked into four large pieces when it hit the floor. *Of course*, it made a comically loud noise that made time stop. As soon as the squabble resumed about me, I trashed my homemade maps, bagged up as much as I could, and made sure I remembered my sketchbook. I didn't know it at the time, but I'd forgotten Whitney's. And that would be a problem.

I slipped out of a side exit I had discovered some weeks earlier and made my way up a short set of stone steps and into the nearby neighborhood. During my time in this abandoned church, I'd made sure to know every nook, every crack, every crevice, every entry, and every exit. I wondered if Dietrich had ever had to escape like this when it was his sanctuary.

Since I was carrying gear, I didn't think I'd be able to

transform. My clothes typically did shift with me, but I wasn't confident that a rucksack would. I made my way to Ortega Street and headed east. I hid out on the campus of Lycée Francais de San Francisco until the bright lights of a police helicopter shined their glare on me. I really needed to transform, but I couldn't leave my stuff behind.

Fuck.

While I was debating my next move, a squadron of bats swarmed the helicopter and damn near made the thing crash. The last thing I needed was a whirlybird falling on my head. More importantly, I didn't want any of my friends getting hurt. It was bad enough that some of them met grisly ends by chopper main rotor blades. The heartening thing, if there could be one, was that the bats had come to my aid without my calling to them or communing with them. They *sensed* I was in danger and responded.

I took advantage of the distraction and headed north along 19th Avenue. The Cypress at Golden Gate old folks' home was nearby. I thought I could find a hiding place among the retirees and tubes of Ben-Gay. I never got there.

A red convertible came flying off Moraga Street and broke into a power slide. The passenger door flung open just as the car screeched to a halt.

"Get in!"

I peered into the vehicle.

Sarah.

"Never mind all that. Get in the fucking car. We don't have time for a huggy-kissy reunion."

Before I could screw my head on straight and come to grips with what was happening, I hopped in the passenger seat. Sarah tromped on the gas and had the car speeding off before I could even get the door shut. There was a predatory look on her perfect face. Her chin was tipped down to her chest, yet her smoldering huntress eyes locked on the street ahead of her. I grabbed the Jesus handle as she deftly maneuvered her car east toward San Francisco.

I looked her up and down. She wore strappy heels, her feet fresh from a pedicure, a tight pencil skirt exposed plenty of leg and hugged her hips, and a loose red blouse with the top two buttons undone showed off her ample décolletage. The tendons and muscles in her right leg rippled, and her toes curled against the hard sole of the shoe as she pressed her foot down harder on the accelerator.

"Where are we going, Sarah?"

"Sit tight, sweetness. Time for talk later. Right now, we need to get the hell out of here."

"How … ?"

"Shush, and let me drive. We're about to have company."

An evil smile curled her ruby red lips. Was that the hint of a fang?

Five SFPD squad cars converged on us from three different directions and took up positions behind us. The sirens blared as the light bars on top of the cars flashed blue and red and blue and red and blue and red. I shielded my eyes while Sarah fished around for a something in the center console. She jerked the wheel left, spun it right, and slipped on a pair of stylish dark sunglasses. Sarah turned her head toward me and slid the sunglasses down her nose and winked.

"Watch the road!"

Sarah turned her attention back to the street in front of her just in time to avoid hitting a bag lady pushing a shopping cart across the street. Cliché, I know, but you can't make this stuff up. I looked out the back window to see if the cops were able to avoid the cart pusher. They weren't so adept at stunt driving. One cruiser clipped the cart and sent its contents flying.

My chauffeur from hell glanced in the rearview mirror and giggled to herself.

"What the fuck are you doing, Sarah? Seriously. Where are we going?"

"Well, we have to lose these cops first."

She was calm, she was cool, she was collected, she was … a vampire? How in the hell did that happen? Once again, my memory failed. Did I cause this? Was it our romp in the shower? I never did figure out how Andrei made me, and he wasn't exactly forthcoming with information. I was pretty sure it didn't just come from a bite or feeding, or else there would be armies of the undead walking the earth just from my body count alone. How in the hell did Sarah *become*? She had been plenty dead when I'd left her behind. But then again, I had to go through quite the process when I "died," rigor mortis and everything. What the fuck did I do?

I racked my brain trying to remember what had happened that night with Andrei. It was all I could do to take my mind off Sarah's haphazard driving. The swerving and air-catching would've made *Streets of San Francisco* stunt drivers throw up. I lost track of where we were and what street we were on back at about *The Fast and the Furious 4*.

The police helicopter had either pureed my bats, or my confederates had broken off the attack, thinking I was clear of danger. I hoped it was the latter as the chopper lit us up with its searchlight.

"Pull over!" blared repeatedly over the helicopter's loudspeakers. Even my OCD counting skills failed me as I lost track of how many cop cars were in pursuit. It was a scene right out of *The Blues Brothers* as Jake and Elwood led hundreds of cops on a high-speed chase through downtown Chicago.

Before I knew it, we were racing along Embarcadero, zigging and zagging to avoid other cars, and staying just ahead of the fleet of cruisers pursuing us.

"Get ready."

"Get ready for what?"

"I'm going to break right toward the water and drop the top on this baby. When I do that, we're going to jump. You know what to do then."

"Are you out of your fucking mind?"

"A little."

Sarah jerked the steering wheel hard to the right and yanked on the emergency brake handle. The car careened toward Pier 33. She hit the button for the convertible top. As soon as the roof cleared the front two seats, she unbuckled our seatbelts.

"Time to fly, chickie!"

Sarah hoisted herself up to a standing position on the driver's seat, jumped out of the car, and transformed into a bat all in one motion. I was enthralled as I watched the shape shifting in real time, never mind her athleticism. It was fascinating to witness. I don't know how she cleared the steering wheel. Her body shrank, clothes and all, as she morphed into a totally different species. So that's what it looks like.

I jumped just before the car hit a corral of water-filled plastic barrels and crashed into the Bay. The rush of wind was a relief as it hit my fur-covered face and body. It took me a few minutes to catch up with Sarah-bat as she flapped her way to Treasure Island. I glanced back to see the helicopter circling and illuminating the water with its searchlight. Numerous squad cars screeched to a stop at the edge of the pier. Sarah's convertible and my stuff sank slowly.

We flew over Perimeter Road and crossed Gateview Avenue. Sarah and I finally alighted on top of City View Storage. We each forced our transformations and shifted back into human form. She pounded the metal surface between us, grabbed my face and kissed me hard, forcing her tongue into my mouth.

Before I let myself melt into the kiss, which was tempting, I recoiled and pushed her away.

"What the fuck, Sarah? What in the actual fuck?"

"That's rich. I just saved your ass. A little gratitude would be nice."

"Yes, you're right, I'm sorry. Thank you, although I am not exactly sure what it is I am thanking you for."

"That was some serious badass stunt driving, wasn't it? Nice outfit, by the way. Looks familiar."

She stepped in to kiss me again, but my right hand rose up to meet her lips and stop the advance in its tracks.

"What's the matter, Be—"

"Nobody calls me BETH!"

"Sorry, Elizabeth. I just thought … well, you're my maker and all. And we had a … "

"A what, Sarah? A moment? Something that shouldn't have happened? A mistake?"

"Is that what I am? A mistake?"

"I don't even know how I … made you."

"Well, you did. I love you. That night … I've never been with a woman before."

"Oh, for fuck's sake. And you still haven't. I'm no woman. I'm something else."

"Yeah, you are, and I am eternally grateful for what you did. I mean, look at me! I'm free! I have never felt more alive! I mean, did you *see* my driving?"

"I was there, Sarah. Yeah, I saw it," I said. *"Scared the shit out of me,"* I mumbled under my breath.

"Yeah, well, you made me, and whether or not you want to accept it, I am in love with you, but I don't answer to you. I don't answer to anyone, really, and I never will again. However, I have been asked to deliver a message."

The light bulb flickered in my head.

"And what does *Andrei* want?"

"Very perceptive, *lover*."

I really didn't care for how that word came out of her face.

"Your meeting has been moved up. Dietrich got wind that your sanctuary was compromised. I don't know how he got word to Andrei … you know, Andrei and I … "

"Yeah, I figured that part out on my own."

"Okay, good. I didn't want there to be any ambiguity. Anyway, Andrei sent me to get you. I was hoping to get there before the cops did. It was just blind luck I found you. I could hear the cops chasing you … "

Sarah was a case in point that we all *become* differently. Certain aspects of her condition were shocking to me. The shape-shifting had come early to her. Her devil-may-care attitude was also a bit strange. From what little I had seen, I started to put a few things together about her and myself, as well. Maybe she was restrained and conservative in life. I was sexually repressed, unfulfilled. My humanity continued to hang on for dear life, while Sarah seemed to shed hers like a snake sheds its skin.

I knew I wasn't done evolving. I wondered if Sarah was.

"What the fuck does Andrei want, Sarah?"

"To meet tonight. Things are getting a little … uncomfortable ... and I think he's planning on leaving the Bay Area. But you called the meet, so he wants to honor that."

"That's awfully big of him."

I didn't have the heart to tell her the only reason I had been attracted to her was because Andrei had tainted her. I was still attracted to her, and I knew deep down that was the only reason. Well, to be fair, she was beautiful. As a vampire, even more so. I noticed it when we were ... driving, and it was distracting now. Her skin, her eyes, her lips ... the taint. It had to be the taint.

"When and where, Sarah?"

"Two a.m. The little pond at Golden Gate Park."

Fuck.

"You have got to be kidding me."

"Nope. That's what he said."

The last thing I needed was another reminder of what had happened to Whitney. And Jonas would be there as well? Andrei had to know. I'm sure that's why he'd picked that particular spot. But what did he hope to gain by getting at me? He had done enough damage, hadn't he?

"You're not coming, are you?"

"Nope, not invited."

"*Good.*"

"'scuse me?"

"Nothing, Sarah. Nothing at all."

I had time until the meeting, and I didn't care to stay any longer with my progeny. If I lingered, I thought there was a good chance I'd do something ill-advised or even stupid. Sarah's infatuation was troublesome, to say the least, and making love to her on top of a metal monthly storage unit was the last thing I wanted to do right now. I sprinted three steps, shifted, and flapped off into the night toward Golden Gate Park.

Don't look back, don't look back, don't look back.

I looked back.

Sarah just stood there, watching me fly away. I felt a tug deep within me that I didn't quite understand. A pang. I don't know how long she lingered. Part of me didn't care, but part of me cared too much.

I took my time flying to Golden Gate Park. After the arriving and shifting, I wandered the paved walking trails, purposely avoiding the pond. When I had been alive, I hadn't appreciated this place. The park was expansive and easy to get lost in. It was one of the most eclectic places I knew of. From the wide-open spaces to the secluded wooded trails, and then from the bison to the carousel, the park had something for everyone. Including thirsty vampires.

As much as I needed to feed, I had other things on my mind, and I eventually found my way to the pond. Sitting down on a large rock, I tossed smaller rocks and pebbles into the water. It wasn't lost on me that everything else cast a reflection. Waterfowl cruised nearby and abruptly changed course as they approached me and realized I wasn't exactly *natural.*

My thoughts wandered to Whitney. That poor kid. She had deserved better. I wondered if she would have lived if I had never crossed her path. Her demise had to be random, yeah? There was no way Dietrich had targeted her because of me. I was racked with guilt.

"Hello, Elizabeth."

"Speak of the devil, and he shall appear. I was just thinking about you, Jonas."

"Oh? Something good, I hope."

"No, not really. You didn't kill Whitney because of me, did you?"

"What? No. Never. I didn't even know you knew her."

"Why didn't you tell me?"

"I didn't know how to."

"It's not like I was some rube who wouldn't believe you, Jonas. We're the same. You lied to me. You played me."

"I know, and I'm sorry. And I can't tell you how sorry I am about Whitney. She was in the wrong place at the wrong time, and the thirst had me. You know how that feels."

"I do, Judgey McJudgerton. I remember all that crap you gave me about the people I killed. You are no better than me. In fact, you're worse. You deny what you are. You hide it."

"And what about you? Christina, Sarah, those people in the boutique in Livermore, the two bros in the hotel room …"

"Oh, you know about that, eh?"

"Yeah. You have a real impulse-control problem, Elizabeth. This bloodbath you've started needs to stop."

"Oh, really? So, I should be more like you? Lying,

hiding, pretending? Tamping it down until the thirst gets you so bad you can't take it anymore? That kid didn't deserve what she got, especially from the likes of a poseur like *you*."

"That was harsh, Elizabeth. I protected you, I looked out for you, I gave you a place to hide."

"And for that, I'm grateful. But your inability to deal with what you are cost that girl her life."

"I know."

Jonas hung his head, looked at the ground, and kicked a rock like a child who was just told he couldn't do something.

"Pouting about it isn't going to bring her back. And where the fuck is Andrei? What time ya got, Jonas?"

"Just past two."

"Bastard. Can't even show up to his own meeting on time."

Jonas and I sat on our own rock and waited. I drew circles in the mud with a stick, while Jonas sat with his legs spread wide and just stared at the ground between his feet. The snap of a twig got my attention. I looked up quickly, half expecting to see Andrei emerging from the trees, but he wouldn't be that clumsy. Instead, I saw the telltale eyeshine of an animal. A raccoon. A growl emanated from my throat, and the fur coat-wearing masked prowler scampered off into the brush.

Andrei appeared on the other side of the pond. He was silent and still. His tailored black suit jacket was fastened with one button. His hands were thrust in his pants' pockets.

His crisp white dress shirt was open at the top two buttons, and it looked silvery in the moonlight. His patent leather dress shoes said tuxedo, but I knew better. Andrei liked them because they were shiny.

"You two should get married," Andrei said matter-of-factly, without much of an accent.

"Funny, Jonas thought you and I should get together."

Andrei carefully circumvented the pond and, with the grace of a ballet dancer, traversed the distance between us. Either he had a thing about water, too, or he just didn't want to get wet. We all know how it went when I fell in. I kinda wished he would have. Then again, I thought I'd finished him in water, so I didn't know how much good it would really do if he did fall in. He was so cocksure of himself.

"So, you two, what shall we talk about? You have questions, yes?"

"Before we get to that, let's get a few things straight. The only reason we're even having this conversation is the fact you showed up out of nowhere to help with Da Rocha. Got it?"

"Fair enough."

Jonas just nodded in agreement. After his hesitation in the fight with the vampire hunter, I wasn't surprised that he didn't have much to say. I figured he'd chime in when he was ready.

"Why me, Andrei? Why anyone like me? Almost every woman you have taken looks like me."

"Victoria," Jonas said.

"What?"

"My daughter. She was six, you sick fuck. Dark hair, green eyes, olive skin." Jonas went away, lost in his memories.

Andrei grinned. He didn't say a word, he just grinned. The bastard just kept on grinning.

"So, you remember Jonas' daughter, do you? Did you creep into her room at night while she slept, too?"

Jonas snapped back to the moment. "You know he did, Elizabeth. There's something wrong with him. He ain't right. I don't know if he was always a pervert or if he became one after he was turned."

Jonas and I regarded Andrei warily. That twisted grin still curled his lips.

"Why Julie?"

"You know why. You didn't listen. I told you to keep a low profile. I told you that you were drawing unnecessary attention to me … I mean, *us*. We survive by staying in the shadows, by taking only what we need. Not by spraying blood. The rest of that night was sport. Bringing your detective friend was an unexpected treat. That was fun."

"Fun? Fun? You call that fun? I ended you."

"Apparently not, my dear." Andrei spread his arms wide in a sweeping motion and bowed, obviously proud of his escape from the lagoon.

"Jonas, you didn't?"

"Did I what?" A look of recognition and understanding flashed across his face. "No! Absolutely not!"

"Swear it?"

"I did not help Andrei that night, I swear."

Although I thought he protested a bit too vehemently, I believed him. Jonas and I had similar motives when it came to Andrei. We both wanted him gone, we both wanted to destroy him for what he had done to us, for what he'd made us do. So, there was no way Jonas had pulled that motherfucker out of the lagoon.

"Running water, my dear, running water. Stagnant, still waters have no effect. And yes, the *becoming* has a different effect on all of us. In most cases, who we *were* is just enhanced. Some of us are liberated, free from our human inhibitions and repressions and oppression. You, my dear Elizabeth, are different. I don't know why. When I first discovered you as a child, oh, did you smell divine. I thought you might be special. You had an aura about you, an electricity I had never experienced before. That's why I waited so long. You needed to reach your potential. I was waiting for you to … *blossom*. All the others were just … playthings."

"Fuck you."

"You really are a twisted fuck."

"Now, now, Detective. Your wife and daughter were quite … *delicious*."

Andrei clapped his hands once, rubbed them together, and laughed the most evil cackle I had ever heard. It wasn't one of those Hollywood put-on evil laughs. This was genuine. He truly was rotten to the core. I wondered if he had been a child molester in his native Hungary. I wondered if he had been discovered and stoned to death in the street.

I really thought Jonas was going to lose his shit when Andrei said the word *delicious*, especially the way he said it. Although Jonas just sat there listening, I could sense the rage building inside him.

"YOU MURDERED MY FAMILY!"

Jonas was now standing, seething and ready to fight. I stood between them, my arms outstretched to keep each one of them at arm's length, like a boxing referee. I almost wanted to see this donnybrook. But we had other priorities.

"As much as I sympathize with you, Jonas, now is not the time for you to work out your demons or settle your differences with Andrei. We both have our issues with him. This is not the time or the place."

"Seventy years, Elizabeth, damn near seventy years … "

I took Jonas's face in both hands and looked him straight in the eyes. "I know, Jonas, I know. You'll get your chance. Right now, this asshole gets a pass because we banded together to fight a common enemy. Da Rocha would've destroyed all three of us. There was no way we could let that happen. You knew what Da Rocha was … what he was capable of."

I had thought I was special because Andrei had selected me. But I was no closer to understanding why I was his type. All I had managed to figure out was that he was a pervert, something straight out of a Nabokov novel. I shuddered to think I was Lolita to his Professor Humbert. I cringed thinking the same of Jonas's daughter, Victoria.

"How do you make a vampire?"

Andrei knew the question was directed at him even though I was still locked in on Dietrich. My tormentor, my molester, my maker hesitated. "How the fuck do you make a vampire, ANDREI?"

The Hungarian child molester stammered and cleared his throat before answering. His accent was in full force when he replied.

"Is simple … process, really. You take blood from human, you make human drink vampire blood, human dies, comes back vampire. Simple."

"Oh, it's that fucking simple, huh, Andrei? I don't remember drinking your blood."

The fact of the matter was, I didn't remember much of anything from that night. I was in and out of consciousness. I remember being trussed up on that giant wooden X. I remember taunting Andrei, trying to get him to make a mistake, something that would give me an opening that would save my life.

Then it hit me like a ton of bricks. The metallic taste. There had been a moment when I'd felt a syrupy liquid in my mouth. That had to be it.

"How did I … ?"

"Sarah? Well, my dear, in your throes of passion with my dear, sweet real estate agent, she must have tasted your blood."

I recalled biting her during our amorous shower, I remembered taking her life … but there was no imprint of her biting me or my allowing her to drink from me. But I must have; that was the only explanation. Other memories flooded the image viewer in my mind, notably Whitney's sneaker-covered foot twitching as Dietrich took that last of her essence. Why couldn't he have turned her?

This meeting needed to reach a conclusion. We weren't getting anywhere rehashing past trespasses. Andrei had provided as much information as he was going to, tonight, anyway. If we didn't conclude our business, Jonas and Andrei would have one fuck of a good fight. And I didn't want to be around for that.

"You two need to go."

"Excuse me, Elizabeth? Who died and made you vampire queen of San Francisco?"

He might have spent the last seventy years as a vampire, but in many ways, Jonas was still just twenty-six.

"Okay, neither one of you is in my good graces right now, so I claim the Bay Area. Andrei can adapt to any environment, I would imagine, and according to him, I draw too much attention to *him*. As for you, Detective, your days of time-hopping and reinventing yourself as a descendent of a bygone San Francisco cop are over. Yes, that's my fault. I'm sorry, I own it. That being said, you need to go, too."

"But where … ?"

My eyes glowed blue. I could see it in the water of the

pond. The three of us cast no reflection in the pool, but the blue glow did.

"Fuck if I know, Jonas; you're a big boy, you figure it out. There isn't enough room for the three of us in San Francisco. I'm sure the cops will be on my head again before long."

My words and electric blue eyes convinced Jonas not to argue with me.

Andrei got the hint as well.

"And so, I bid you *au revoir*."

Motherfu …

Before I could utter another word, Andrei was gone on the wind or into the wind.

"You can come out now, Sarah!"

My creation stepped out of the darkness and into the moonlight. She was a bit embarrassed and acted shy. I didn't quite understand the act.

"How did you … ? I didn't make a sound."

Was Sarah spying for Andrei? Was she looking for me?

"You need to go."

"But I need you, Be—"

"It is so important to your future that you don't complete that sentence. Nobody, nobody calls me Beth!"

I flew to Sarah and grabbed her by the face. Spittle flew from my mouth as I hissed at her.

"You. Need. To. Go. NOW!"

I pushed her face with enough force to knock her off balance. She rubbed her chin and ran off into the trees.

Jonas and I stood there, stunned by Sarah's sudden appearance. We stared at the space she had just occupied.

After a long while, I finally softened my disposition and said to Jonas, "Walk with me."

I inserted my hand and arm through his, and we took to the trails of Golden Gate Park. My dear, sweet detective and I walked for the rest of the night, hardly saying a word. The nocturnal creatures barely registered. A gentle breeze rustled the leaves on the trees. The lawn bowling courts, Hippie Hill, and Robin Williams Meadow were eerily silent. Even the bison were quiet. After strolling to the edges of the expanse and back again, I said, "Where will you go?"

"I had a feeling it was going to come to this. I knew once my police job was compromised, I would have a hard time with everything. There was no going back after that night at Local Edition. I tried to salvage it, but too much damage had already been done. You know how it goes. Cops hate murderous cops, especially weird ones. I think I might head to Las Vegas."

"You might fit right in."

We chuckled over the implications of a vampire detective prowling the streets of Sin City. We also talked about what I might do, where I might find sanctuary. I knew I would head to the art store in North Beach after this conversation was over. There was no way in hell I was going to tell Dietrich about it.

"I wish things could have been different between us, Elizabeth, I really do."

"I know."

Jonas opened his mouth to say something else, but I put my index finger to his lips.

"Don't."

With that, Detective Sergeant Jonas Dietrich and his trench coat fluttered off into the waning moments of the late summer San Francisco night. I found some open ground and sprinted. Within five strides, I shifted and took to the sky. I flapped my way to what I hoped would just be a temporary hiding place. I landed on the roof and made my way inside. The lower level I had discovered during my search for such places wasn't ideal, but it would have to do for now.

Before I could close my eyes and enter my catatonic state, Blackfoot appeared at my feet and walked up my legs to my lap. She plopped and curled into a ball.

"How in the hell … ?"

I blanked out to the soft sounds of her purrs.

CHAPTER XXVIII

Now, every one of my other hiding places, every last one, had been completely abandoned or somewhat forsaken. Foot traffic was nonexistent, except for the two hapless graffiti artists back at the rail yard. Even the crypt in the cemetery in Livermore was secluded. Well, my dumbass self had found somewhere to hide that was far less than ideal. Evening shoppers at the art supply store were going to be a problem. You would have thought that while investigating ingress and egress and security, I would have at least checked the fucking store hours.

I rose to meet the night only to find Blackfoot several steps ahead of me and long gone. She came and went as she pleased, and I really didn't understand why her ability to find me still surprised me. The next time I needed to change hiding places, I wouldn't be shocked if that damn cat was sitting there, waiting for me.

While I sat in the dark waiting for the patrons to clear out and the store to close, I thought about the events of the previous night. Where would Andrei go? Would Jonas actually go to Las Vegas? Had I made an enemy of Sarah? Nah, she'd get over it.

Right; just like I'd gotten over what Andrei had done to me.

The last time I had parted company with Andrei in dramatic fashion was by my choice. I still didn't know how he'd found the strength to escape his watery grave. He was like a bad penny. He just kept showing up. I had a sinking feeling he would continue to. The meeting was amicable, but I'd learned more about Andrei than I'd ever wanted to know just by studying his mannerisms and reactions. He really was a sick fuck, and I felt ... dirty. It was his blood that ran through my veins. It was his preternatural energy that had given me this *life*, this unnatural existence. And that made me ill.

Sarah was another issue altogether. I rejected her. Her maker pushed her away. She was infatuated with me, and that was not something I was prepared to deal with. Not now, at least. Something deep down told me I would have to deal with her eventually. I also had no idea how Andrei had made me; I mean, his explanation made some kind of sense, but I had no recollection of actually tasting his blood. I had no clue how I'd turned Sarah. Most of that experience was a blur, too. From an unexpected attraction to a woman to ending her and raiding her closet, I didn't really remember much.

Speaking of closet raiding, I was sure I looked like hell.

There were still so many things I didn't know. What more could I do and be? The electric blue eyes were still a mystery to me. Taking the blood of a sanctified vampire hunter had something to do with it, I was sure. But I wasn't sure what, or what it meant, or what I was supposed to do with it. I was pretty sure it wasn't a MAG light.

What I did know was that this would probably be the only day I spent in the basement of an art supply store. I needed to find something more secluded and somewhat long-term. Without a job or any reliable source of income, I wasn't about to drop an apartment rental application. Oh, yeah, and I was dead.

Sarah could've helped. Little Miss Real Estate Agent. I smacked myself in the forehead with the heel of my palm. I'm sure we could've teamed up and found a righteous place to hide out. I wondered if she remembered that part of her former life. I wondered if she still had a human part. I hoped she wasn't just a shell of her former self acting out of instinct.

The store above me finally was quiet, and I decided it was safe for me to ascend to the street.

Did I mention I was thirsty?

I climbed out of the secret lower level to the subfloor. As I slid out of the tunnel in the wall, I heard some hustling and bustling in the racks. A young man in his early twenties was restocking and rearranging the shelves as he was preparing to close up shop for the night. God, I was stupid. I should have known this. Rarely do shopkeepers shoo out the last of the customers, lock the doors, and head out for the night. There's always something left to do after the last of the customers spill out into the street.

That was okay. This was the last night that ... what did it say on his name tag? Oh, yeah, Jamal. This was the last night Jamal was going to have to worry about getting stuck locking up, when, what did he say? Oh, yeah, when he had "shit to do." Well, all he had to do now was finish bleeding to death.

My eyes glowed blue as the crimson blood flowed into my thirsty mouth ... so many colors ... burnt umber, turquoise, violet. I thought my enhanced vision was cycling through the spectrum before I realized that I had spaced out on a display of acrylic paint color swatches.

Maybe I would never solve the mystery of the electric azure orbs glowing in my sockets. What I did know was that it would take folks some time to find Jamal. Unfortunately, where I stashed him meant I couldn't use the art supply store as a refuge anymore. I'd spent how long in the abandoned church? And now, I burned a hiding place in less than twenty-four hours? Good job. I seriously needed to get better at all of this. It made me cringe to think of it, but there were several reasons why Andrei had lasted this long.

The last thing I wanted to do was rehash anything to do with that asshole, but until I came along, he really had it all down to a science. Not that I gave a shit that I'd ruined the framework of his existence; I had tried to end him. But his MO, his targeting, the ritual nature of his killings and feedings ... I wondered if I could ever develop that kind of style. I was a killer, a nocturnal predator, and there was an awful lot about it that I enjoyed. But the pathology that went with my maker ... I still didn't understand it all. He'd been coy when we'd parted company, and he'd left Dietrich and me believing he was nothing more than an undead pervert. Andrei hadn't done much to dispel that notion.

CHAPTER XXIX

Four months later

Since the entire Bay Area was my territory, in theory, anyway, I thought I might expand to the other side of the bridge. Berkeley, Oakland, San Leandro. I could go anywhere, really.

With my new sanctuary in San Francisco secure, exploring sounded like a good idea. So much of my time had been spent between Livermore, Pacifica, and The City dealing with Andrei and Dietrich that I had all but forgotten about the municipalities I could visit.

Arising from my crypt on a cold late November night, I eventually made my way to the Powell Street BART station and just caught the last train of the night with enough time to transfer to a Berkeley-bound train. The nights were getting longer, and I couldn't have been happier. This was what I had been waiting for. Colder temperatures, longer nights. The endless summer had finally given way, and I was enjoying the change in seasons. Halloween was fun. I fit right in.

I boarded the train and sat in a back-corner seat, spending my two train rides watching what few late-night BART riders there were. An older gentleman who was undoubtedly homeless slept across the seat reserved for handicapped patrons. The train car rocked side to side, and I thought he would roll right onto the floor, but he was perfectly balanced in his heavy surplus army jacket, snow pants, and well-worn work boots.

A young couple heading home after a date sat in the backward facing seats. He was in a dark blue suit, and she wore a tight-fitting fire-engine-red dress. He was drunk. He threw up all over her. I chuckled softly to myself as they fought.

Riders came and went, a few staying on just for a stop or two, others a little longer.

After changing trains in west Oakland and getting off at the Downtown Berkeley station, I wandered the streets of the historic college town. I strolled south along Oxford Street and east on Bancroft Way. I wandered north on Piedmont past Berkeley Law, the Haas School of Business, and the Greek Theater. The students were off for Thanksgiving break, so I had many of the campus streets and walkways to myself. I broke left on Hearst and made the loop two more times before heading to Telegraph. It was as if I were compelled to head south.

A police car, an ambulance, and a fire engine sped past, light bars flashing and sirens wailing. Something bad had happened somewhere. Someone once said, "No one's ugly after two a.m." I was pretty sure someone also said, "Nothing good happens after two a.m."

After all that I'd gone through with cars and hitchhiking, you'd think I would have flown. The ability to transform into a flying creature had solved quite a few of my transportation problems, but I wanted to feel *human*. Just for a little while. I had enjoyed the train ride, and the walk was cathartic, despite the nagging, insistent pull I'd developed. I needed to clear my head and wrap it around some things. I was still a baby, but I needed to grow up fast.

My pace quickened as I felt an increasing sense of urgency. I had no idea where I was going or why. The businesses along Telegraph barely registered as I zipped past them. The Pho restaurant, the Ethiopian spot, even the Goth clothing store didn't raise an eyebrow as I sped along. I did make a mental note to go back to the Goth boutique later.

I crossed Parker and Carleton and Derby as I continued traveling south. I passed a school and crossed Stuart, Russell, and Oregon, and then turned left at Ashby. I crossed Colby and made a right on Regent Street. All this walking was eating up the night, and I still had no idea where I was going or why. Sunrise was coming, and I needed a place to crash for the day.

Alta Bates Summit Medical Center.

Hospital Drive to Colby to Ashby to Regent. Hospital Drive to Colby to Ashby to Regent. Hospital Drive to Colby to Ashby to Regent. And back around the other way twice. I was obsessing. I wanted to count something. I drifted toward the emergency room entrance, adjacent to the rest of the facility. There was that splinter in my brain again.

And just like that, it was gone. The pull, the itch in my gray matter, gone. I didn't know if I should be angry or what. Confusion and frustration set in, two feelings I did not like at all. I screamed at the sky. The reply was a deep rumble of thunder. "That's it? That's all I get?"

I didn't know what to expect, really. It had been quite some time since I'd brought a thunderstorm down upon San Francisco with my emotions. Since I wasn't in a life-or-death situation, and I wasn't confronted by people I hated, my cries brought forth what amounted to a burp from the cloudy purple skies.

I thrust my hands into the pockets of my wool overcoat, more out of habit than the need for warmth, and pounded my way around Berkeley, the soles of Sarah's thigh-high suede boots echoing off the cement of the uneven and cracked sidewalks.

An unfulfilled college student would be found in a dumpster in an alley with her throat torn out tomorrow morning, or the next day, or whatever day trash day fell on.

I didn't have much of an MO yet, but I'd certainly figured out my taste and type. The thirst was still maddening, but after a few months of working on my willpower and meditating, I had whittled my feedings down to once or twice per week. I didn't think I'd ever get to Andrei's infrequency. I enjoyed it too much. I was also getting better at hiding the bodies.

After disposing of … what did she say her name was … oh, yeah … Sienna, I hopped the last BART train and headed back to San Francisco. My latest hiding spot was pure genius, if you ask me, but you're out of your fucking mind if you think I'm going to tell you where to find it.

CHAPTER XXX

My OCD was starting to kick in and the thirst had me. The very next night after my jaunt to Berkeley, I felt compelled to take BART again and go back. The draw was stronger this time, and the thirst was a scratchy burn in the back of my throat. Sienna should have slaked my thirst for a few days at least, but this felt more like the summer days when I couldn't control my ravenous inclinations.

The nagging was a knot in the pit of my stomach, tightening with each passing moment. I paid no attention to the other riders. The gentle rocking of the train was imperceptible, and my thoughts were locked in on one thing. It was as if a magnet were pulling me back to where I'd been the night before. I stared out the grimy window and did my best not to count everything.

I changed trains as I had the night before. Despite the

ever-tightening knot, I didn't move when the train pulled into the station, but I hopped off before the doors closed. Not that I couldn't get off at the next one, but I wanted the shortest walk possible. The night before I'd wandered, I'd circled, and then the draw had hit me. This night was different. When I rose to meet the night, the pull was already there. And this was where it wanted me to go.

It was the oddest thing. As much as I felt the need to find Andrei and exact revenge for what he had done to me, I'd never felt *drawn* to him. I wasn't drawn to Christina or Sarah either; they had just happened to cross my path. True, I couldn't resist either of them, and I also couldn't resist the force that was pulling me along a path similar to the one I'd walked the night before.

Instead of circling the University of California campus this time, I made a beeline south from the BART station. I made my way to Telegraph and shot straight south to Ashby. I crossed against lights, and I elbowed pedestrians out of the way as my pace became more urgent. My thoughts were frantic, desperate but unfocused. What would I find at the end of this road tonight? Another hunter? Andrei?

Staring at the ground as I walked, I counted the seams in the concrete slabs on the sidewalks between the BART station and the Alta Bates Summit Medical Center. The number flew away on the cold November wind when I realized where I was. Loose patients in wheelchairs waited for rides or took smoke breaks. Nobody noticed that I didn't cast a reflection in the mirrored windows. Standing on a triangular corner on Colby, I stared at the building, perplexed. The night before the draw had dissipated rather quickly. Not this night. It persisted and grew stronger with each passing second.

I paced from Ashby to Bateman Mall Park on the edge of Hospital Drive and lost count of how many times I made that back-and-forth trip in front of Alta Bates. An ambulance pulled up and hauled a victim of an incident into the emergency room entrance. The EMTs were hustling and wore harried, worried looks on their faces.

The pull just wouldn't let go, regardless of how long I stared or how many times I walked back and forth in front the medical center. Something was amiss. Something was wrong. The cold November wind carried something foul. Instead of pounding back to Ashby this time, I took a left on Hospital Drive.

Just as I approached a loading dock, someone carrying a bundle emerged from a side door to the building. The person was familiar, too familiar. It was dark, and I couldn't make her out right away. My eyes had trouble adjusting because of the light coming from inside the doorway and a street lamp across the way. I couldn't focus. The pull, however, was the strongest yet. Just as she was about to come into full view, I was blinded by the headlights of a box truck that had just pulled away from the loading dock. I barely ducked out of the way before the damn thing turned me into a hood ornament.

My quarry was halfway down the street and almost to

Regent Street when I finally regained my vision. She was clutching the bundle tightly to her bosom as she strutted with a sense of urgency. The pull dragged me along the street in pursuit.

Then I heard a noise that froze me in my tracks. The wail of a baby. The woman I pursued was swinging her bundle wildly from side to side as she picked up speed. The baby she carried was agitated by the movement.

As I chased after her, I started to realize what was amiss. The skin crawled on my back and the hairs on my neck stood on end; an icy chill slithered from my tailbone to the base of my skull.

Her clothes.

Her scent.

Her figure.

Her hair.

"HEY!"

She froze at the corner of Regent and Hospital. She turned her head slowly and looked over her left shoulder.

Julie.

She turned to face me in an aggressive stance with a newborn baby swaddled and cradled in her arms. A devilish grin curled her lips. Moonlight and street lamps shone on her porcelain white face and revealed her fangs.

No.

Not possible.

"You're dead. I watched you die. I held you in my arms as you died."

Julie, or the Julie-thing, just stood there. A fat drop of blood dripped from the impossibly sharp, elongated right canine onto the baby's forehead. Julie, looking up at me with wild malice in her eyes, licked the drop from the child's forehead. A moan of ecstasy escaped as she dragged her tongue over the baby's soft skin. After she licked her lips again, she tilted her head back and laughed. It wasn't Julie's playful laugh or her bubbleheaded-bleached-blonde giggle. It was something else. Something rotten.

Before I could say another word, Julie turned on a stiletto heel and took off running down Regent.

I couldn't move. I was stunned. I wanted to chase after her. But it was as if I were glued to the spot. *"What the fuck did I just see?"*

After a long moment, I finally mustered the gumption to chase after her. Julie turned right on Webster at East Bay Pediatrics and continued north. Her cackling echoed off the buildings. I thought it would be easy to catch her since she was carrying a baby and I was running unencumbered, but I was wrong. Her speed was astonishing. She led me on quite the merry chase as we crossed Hillegass and Benvenue. She broke left and disappeared between two buildings before we reached the corner.

I slowed to a walk as I tried to re-acquire my target. Every noise was a baby fussing or cooing. I couldn't focus. I wandered between the buildings. And then a voice from above.

"Hey, Beth!"

I looked up. Julie was standing on the flat roof of a one-story building. She leaned over the edge with the baby in her arms. The infant was wailing.

"Nobody calls me Be—"

Julie was giggling her bubbleheaded-bleached-blonde giggle as she turned and ran across the rooftop. I broke from my spot between the structures and ran back to the street. I took a hard left and sprinted to the corner, hoping to cut Julie off at the pass. *The pass? Who the fuck says that?* Just as I got to the corner, a red convertible with the top down roared out of nowhere and screeched to a halt just before the intersection. 'The passenger door was flung open; Julie darted in from my left and hopped into the car, the infant close to her chest. Both driver and passenger shot me nasty, devil-may-care death stares. I finally got a good look at the driver.

Sarah.

Motherfucker.

Where the hell did this car come from? Sarah's went into the drink and almost took both of us with it. This was not the time for a discussion about her automobile acquisition skills.

Sarah tromped on the gas, smoking the tires. She cranked the wheel hard to the left as she willed her car to make a U-turn in the heavy traffic. The backend threatened to fishtail, but Sarah managed to regain control, and she hit the accelerator and zoomed off into the night with Julie and the baby. I just stood there. I couldn't believe what I'd just witnessed.

Julie was alive. Well, that was a relative term. She'd also teamed up with … with … SARAH? Andrei had to be behind this.

After several minutes, I leaned against the nearest building and put my back to it. I wrapped an arm around my stomach, rested my chin in my hand and my elbow on the opposite wrist. I raised my right leg, bent my knee, and placed the sole of my right foot against the brick.

"Well, fuck."

-The End-

LOOK FOR THE DARK TERROR
BOOK #3 - COMING SOON!

That sly grin curled my lips and revealed my fangs. My eyes burned an electric blue I still didn't quite understand.

"I'm taking the baby, Andrei."

"Oh, are you now?"

"Yeah, and there's not one goddamn thing you can do to stop me."

"Tsk, tsk, tsk. Still with the language. When I first discovered you as a child, I had such high hopes for you, such …"

"Shut the fuck up. Seriously. Do you ever shut up?"

And with that, I directed my winged posse to attack Andrei with impunity. He threw his arms in front of his eyes in an instinctive protective manner, before disappearing in a poof of fog. While he was distracted and fighting off my pals, I scooped up the baby and headed for the exit. Sarah made a move to rise to her feet. Her lips were pulled back, her fangs were bared and she hissed at me. It was a weak hiss, it was more like a leak.

"Bitch, don't. Where are your car keys?"

"I-i-i-n the ignition."

"Good answer."

The bats continued to swirl about and they flew alongside me like a fighter escort as I headed out into the night. My protectors dispersed as I broke the telepathic connection and headed for Sarah's BMW.

ABOUT THE AUTHOR

Jerry Knaak, a 10-year U.S. Navy veteran, has been writing professionally for 25 years.

A native of Rochester, N.Y., he enlisted in the Navy upon graduation from Edison Tech in 1987. Since serving as a radio and television personality in with Armed Forces Radio and Television at Naval Air Station Keflavik, Iceland, and as a writer for Naval Aviation News magazine in Washington, D.C., Jerry has worked with the Oakland Raiders professional football team for the past 17 years. He has produced thousands of articles for online publication during his career. After 16 years in digital media, he is now serving as the team historian. Knaak started his sports writing career with Baltimore Football Weekly, covering the Baltimore Stallions of the Canadian Football League.

Jerry currently lives in Northern California with his wife Angi and son Noah, three cats, a dog, numerous koi fish, and any number of vagrant spiders and lizards. His oldest son, William, is attending college in Florida.

When he's not writing gritty tales of terror or

researching gridiron heroics, Jerry enjoys reading, watching movies and good serial television, and exercise. He is also an avid blogger and hosts a regular podcast.

The Dark Truth is his first novel.

ACKNOWLEDGMENTS

I would like to thank:

My family – Noah and Angi – for their support and encouragement throughout this journey, and my oldest son, William as he finishes his first year of college … my editor Jodi McDermitt, who continues to make sure I write coherent sentences … Sofia Avalos, for not only supporting my writing endeavors but for helping me get back down to my fighting weight … Tony Gonzales, for the fantastic promotional photos, it's not easy making this mug look good … my cousins, who have not only bought and read the book, but who have helped in numerous other ways … beta readers Kristi and Fudgie, who caught typos in *The Dark Truth* at the eleventh hour … everyone who purchased and enjoyed *The Dark Truth* … Mockingbird Books in Tracy, Calif., for my first booking … Modesto Barnes & Noble for my first B&N shelving and signing event ... and of course, my publisher, Trifecta Publishing House – thank you Diana, Doug and Lori.

CPSIA information can be obtained
at www.ICGtesting.com
Printed in the USA
FSHW04n0015180418
47074FS